TALES from BUSH HOUSE

Collected and edited by
Hamid Ismailov, Marie Gillespie and Anna Aslanyan

HERTFORDSHIRE PRESS

First published in 2012
by Hertfordshire Press
Suite 125, 43 Bedford Street
Covent Garden, WC2 9HA, United Kingdom

© 2012 Hamid Ismailov, Marie Gillespie, Anna Aslanyan

Typeset by Aleksandra Vlasova

Printed in Turkey by IMAK OFSET

All rights reseved. No part of this book may be reprinted or reproduced or utilised in any form or by any electronic, mechanical, or other means, now known or hereafter invented, including photocopying and recording, or in any information storage or retrieval system, without permission in writng from the publishers.

British Library Catalogue in Publication Data
A catalogue record for this book is available from the British Library

Library of Congress in Publication Data
A catalogue record for this book has been requested

ISBN 978-0-9557549-7-5

British Broadcasting Corporation

Contents

Prologue 04

Introduction 07

Chapter One
On Air: "Good Thing It Isn't TV" 15

Chapter Two
Off Air: "Look Neither Eager nor Flurried" 40

Chapter Three
History Live: "Would You Lend Us the Commando Brigade?" 72

Chapter Four
Rubbing Shoulders: "Sorry, Where Did You Say You Were King of?" 106

Chapter Five
Tower of Babel: "A Mini-Version of the British Empire" 135

Two Poems 160

Epilogue 164

Acknowledgements 169

Prologue

This book ends with a poem. Therefore, to explain the idea behind it, the best thing to do may be to start it with a poem too.

> From my childhood spent in a clay hut of a mountainous Uzbek village to my life in the Soviet Moscow in a shanty two-piece flat, I used to dream of a grand house with a marble staircase.
> That dream was quite regular;
> Without any intention I dreamt again and again of that house with marble columns and stairs, leading upwards.
> I read Freud, I read Jung, I read other interpreters, trying to understand: what does that dream mean?
> A gypsy fortune-teller told me in Sverdlovsk: "You'll have a grand house in your future, a house with marble columns and stairs leading upwards."
> My life is nearly ending, but living in an ex-council town house, I often think, what was that empty promise about, that dream which never came true?
> But dreams aside, all of a sudden I realised that over the last 18 years, I spent almost a third of my life in that house with marble columns and stairs leading upwards.
> I had never noticed it until we were asked to leave it.
> Bush House - the Noah's Ark of nations,
> The runway where voices take off and fly over Earth, the kingdom where echoes of the dead are kept alive, the thinking brain, the watchful eye, the sharp tongue and the caring heart of meridians, Bush House – an English pub, an Uzbek chay-khana, a Spanish tavern, an African hut, a Russian kabak, where views and opinions fly around, vibrating the globe, Bush House – a cold mirror in front of that old, beautiful and furious world...
> A house of my imperceptibly fulfilled dream...

When in November 2010 Gwyneth Williams, the then director of the English World Service, invited me for a cup of tea and suggested that I become the first ever writer-in-residence at the BBC World Service, one of her requirements was to maintain the legendary culture of Bush House. After being there for over 70 years, the World Service is moving to its new headquarters. Bush House will cease to exist as a broadcasting centre. The poem above is about the feelings which, undoubtedly, I share with thousands of my unsung colleagues. Bush House has been a heroic place from the very beginning. Georgi Markov, a Bulgarian dissident writer, was killed with a poisoned umbrella for his truthful programmes made here. People like Michael Gardner, Alan Johnson, Mirwais Jalil, Mohiddin Olimpour and many other epic figures used to work here. On the other hand, many great writers left their footprints on the stairs and carpets of this building: George Orwell, V. S. Naipaul and Derek Walcott among them.

Bush House is so rich in history that I thought it should be somehow preserved in some form or another. Then the idea of a folkloric book about it came to my mind. In my announcement to my colleagues I said:

"The great history of Bush is coming to an end. But as one famous philosopher said, 'Humanity should part with its past cheerfully.' So should we.

As the World Service writer-in-residence I'm collecting anecdotes about life in Bush House, which could be published as a book. Every one of you must have at least one funny story (if not more). Don't keep it to yourself, email it to me. Let's celebrate the legacy of Bush House with a witty, funny, joyful and cheerful book, written by all of us."

The take-off was amazing. People started sending me their memories, short stories, some funny, some serious. I found my closest supporter and collaborator in the face of Professor Marie Gillespie of The Open University, who was with me throughout the whole project. Marie is a renowned scholar of the World Service. She directed a large research project on it, as part of which she organised a number of seminars devoted to the writers and literature of the World Service. These seminars helped to spark the idea of a writer-in-residence. Marie is one of the best sources of knowledge about Bush House. She and Anna Aslanyan have shaped and edited the book. Their contribution to it is enormous and I am extremely grateful to them. Without them the book wouldn't exist.

The book would also never be possible without our contributors, raconteurs, narrators, who shared their stories with us and whom I thank for their time and generosity.

During Uzbek celebrations the host is usually invisible and, following this tradition, I haven't included my own stories in this book. But in order not to sound too detached I'd better finish with an anecdote from our service.

In the early 1990s, when the Central Asian Service had just been set up, we used to translate quite a lot of news from English. The newsroom's usual way of writing stories at that time was never to mention names in the first sentence, using instead openings like this: "The President of Russia and the President of the USA met today. Mr Yeltsin and Mr Clinton discussed the issues..." Once, on a night shift, an Azeri colleague who worked for our Central Asian Russian programme received a script from the newsroom: "A member of the Kyrgyz Parliament, Jokorgu Kenesh, died today at the age of 48." He started to translate it into Russian: "A member of the Kyrgyz Parliament, Mr Jokorgu Kenesh, died today at the age of 48." But the second sentence was quite confusing because it went: "Mr Mambetov had a fatal accident in the capital of Kyrgyzstan, Bishkek." So the Azeri colleague looked at the third sentence, which made perfect sense: "The Member of Parliament used to do so and so, he was well known for this and that, etc."

"What is this Mr Mambetov doing in the report?" the colleague thought with a certain deal of irritation. "These newsroom writers know nothing about our countries – they only muck everything up!" Still outraged, she irreversibly changed Mr Mambetov for Mr Jokorgu Kenesh, not suspecting that Jokorgu Kenesh, which translates as Supreme Council, was the name of the Kyrgyz Parliament.

Thus that night the entire Kyrgyz Parliament was buried alive by my innocent colleague.

For all its magnanimous seriousness Bush House was a funny place – I hope you will discover that while reading this book.

Hamid Ismailov

Introduction

"A tale never loses in the telling"

Tales From Bush House is a collection of short narratives about working lives, mostly real and comic, sometimes poignant or apocryphal, gifted to the editors by former and current BBC World Service employees. They are tales from inside Bush House – the home of the World Service since 1941 – escaping through its marble-clad walls at a time when its staff begin their departure to new premises in Portland Place. In July 2012, the grand doors of this imposing building will close on a vibrant chapter in the history of Britain's most cosmopolitan organisation.

The British public know very little about the workings of the World Service, except for insomniacs who listen to it in the middle of the night when Radio 4 transmutes into World Service radio, and intrepid travellers for whom it is often a lifeline. This is a great shame because in 2014, for the first time, the World Service will be funded through the UK licence fee system, which has hitherto only supported the BBC's domestic services, rather than through a grant-in-aid from the budget of the Foreign and Commonwealth Office. It remains to be seen exactly how this change will affect the distinctive culture of broadcasting at the World Service, but there is no doubt that something precious will be lost. So this is a timely book. In its collective authorship, it documents the cultural diversity of the organisation, showing how the extraordinary people who worked there, and the magnificent, chaotic building they shared, shaped one another.

We use the word "tales" to signal that this is a book that mixes genres – ethnographic and folkloric stories, oral histories and jokes. Recounting tales involves an intricate relationship between talking and telling – as in the working life of a broadcaster. A book of tales, written as if recorded viva voce, seemed appropriate for an international organisation that has, for most of its history, been dedicated to radio broadcasting, where the spoken and written word have long wrestled. Radio is a distinctive and often neglected medium in this age that favours vision and the visual

– especially television and the Internet. Its essential quality lies in the evocative power and intimacy of the human voice, which captures and wraps a tale in its very own personal and distinctive idiom, yet is capable of conjuring a universal appeal. Over the last 70 years, human voices, speaking in many tongues, emanating from Bush House and travelling on the airwaves across the globe, have forged a loyal and intimate connection with audiences overseas. The polyglot human voices spilling out of Bush House have been the foundation of the respect that the BBC World Service has enjoyed – and this book is a tribute to them.

The term "tales" connotes folk and fairy tales. While there are no obvious goblins, elves, gnomes, giants or princesses in *Tales From Bush House*, insiders will be able to cast real-life characters in these roles – as did the talks writer Nick Rankin in his pantomime *Malice in Blunderland*. Broadcast at Christmas 1995, it was a 45-minute programme parodying the BBC's Orwellian marketing newspeak. But Rankin was far from alone in using experiences of working at Bush House to pen comic fictions. One of the most striking aspects of Bush House culture is its effervescent humour and cosmopolitan creativity. These qualities of character and of working life go hand in hand. Writing on air and off air are, for many inhabitants of Bush House, parallel aspects of a writing life, influencing each other mostly positively – as the work of my long time collaborators and friends, Hamid Ismailov and Zinovy Zinik, among others, testifies. The question of writing on air and off air was explored at a series of three "witness seminars" (a special form of oral history), entitled Bush Writers, at The Open University in 2009 [1]. These seminars, co-organised with Zinovy Zinik and Sophie West, were entertaining as well as moving events, as Bush writers came together to share revealing testimonies about their working and writing lives. We debated the practices and ethics of journalism, compared and contrasted journalistic and creative writing. We explored the turmoil and pleasures of exile, of being a foreigner, the ways in which creative work can sometimes mend psychic ruptures and sometimes exacerbate them to powerful creative effect. In this book we have complemented the rich material gathered by Hamid Ismailov's call for anecdotes to all the BBC World Service staff with the testimonies presented at the witness seminars. The collection also draws on material from a research project entitled "Tuning In: Diasporic Contact Zones at the BBC World Service". This project, funded by the Arts and Humanities Research Council, was part of a wider programme of research on diasporas, migration and identities. Through the prism of the World Service, we documented and analysed, often collaboratively with Bush House broadcasters, the dynamics of cosmopolitan culture at Bush House, historically and comparatively.[2]

1. See http://www8.open.ac.uk/researchprojects/diasporas/projects/bush-writers-1940-2012 (accessed 30 May 2012). See also "Poets at Bush House: The BBC World Service", Modern Poetry in Translation, 22, 2003 (special issue, guest ed. Daniel Weissbort) and "Writers at Bush House", Wasafiri: International Contemporary Writing, 68, 2011 (special issue, guest ed. Marie Gillespie).

2. See "Tuning In: Diasporic Contact Zones at the BBC World Service" (AHRC reference AH/ES58693/1), the project based at The Open University, directed by Marie Gillespie. The publications arising from this collaborative project provide the most comprehensive body of academic research to date on the BBC World Service. Details can be found at http://www8.open.ac.uk/researchprojects/diasporas/ (accessed 30 May 2012).

Bush House is a polyglot microcosm of 20th century intellectual and creative diasporas: a globally pre-eminent cross-cultural contact zone. Successive waves of exiled writers, dissident intellectuals and refugee poets have flocked here to earn a living by giving voice to BBC broadcasts in many tongues, meanwhile honing their personal craft as writers, often in more than one language. The story begins in 1939, when the BBC Empire Service, as it was then, was re-named the BBC Overseas Service (it only became the World Service in 1988). The embryonic Ministry of Information asked the BBC to monitor enemy propaganda in dozens of languages. Dissidents who fled to London, the centre of the fight against fascism in Europe, found their linguistic skills in high demand. By October 1941 nearly 250 bulletins in 30 languages were being monitored daily by 500 foreign language specialists, who listened to the war unfold and translated its intrigues, surprises and tragedies. Many of these gifted amateurs progressed from radio and press monitoring to begin broadcasting to their compatriots in their respective languages. Among them were such distinguished intellectuals in exile, later luminaries of British and international postwar culture, as the art critic Ernst Gombrich, the publisher, philanthropist and political commentator George Weidenfeld, the playwright and translator Martin Esslin and the brilliant linguist Anatol Goldberg, who would become the BBC's most popular voice in Russian. By 1942, the BBC was broadcasting in 45 languages[3].

The loyal collegial friendships that developed at Bush House were an essential part of the culture. Some were legendary. George Orwell, for example, was a talks producer (1941--43) working in close partnership with an Indian Muslim called Zulfaqar Ali Bokahari, a programme organiser (1940--65) for Talking to India. The programme broadcast commentaries, poetry, plays and music, targeting anti-fascist propaganda at India's intellectual and cultural elites. Orwell's scripts were translated into Hindustani and read out, or "ventriloquised" by Bokhari among other Indians at the BBC. The aim was to secure the allegiance of Indians to Britain's war effort. This was a time of fraught Indo-British relations. The Quit India Movement was taking off and prominent Indian nationalists were allying with the Axis powers. The right kind of diaspora voices emanating from the imperial metropolis were, as the BBC knew only too well, a tool of enormous cultural and political power. Accent, tone and cadence were essential to conveying a British perspective, without compromising the BBC's reputation for impartiality. Orwell may have regarded his two years at the Eastern Service as "wasted years" but he profited enormously from them – not least as a result of working alongside some leading intellectuals and writers, including Mulk Raj Anand, Balraj Sahni and Una Marson. And his Room 101 is thought to have been inspired by his time at Bush House.

3. For further details see: Gerard Mansell, *Let Truth Be Told: 50 Years of BBC External Broadcasting*, London: Weidenfeld and Nicolson, 1982; John Tusa, *A World in Your Ear: Reflections on Changes*, London: BBC, 1992; Marie Gillespie, "Diasporic Creativity: Refugee Intellectuals, Exiled Poets and Corporate Cosmopolitanism at the BBC World Service", in K Knott and S McLoughlin (eds), *Diasporas: Concepts, Intersections, Identities*, London: Zed Books, 2010: 236—243; Marie Gillespie and Alban Webb, *Diasporas and Diplomacy: Corporate Cosmopolitanism at the BBC World Service*, London: Routledge, 2012.

One important aim of "Tuning In" was to plug the gap in public and academic knowledge about Bush House and to understand its unique brand of corporate cosmopolitanism. Bush House has long provided spaces of cultural encounter, translation, representation and performance, and we have much still to learn from its history. But being a cross-cultural contact zone ensures neither a sense of community nor one of cohesion. Bush House, like any large organisation, is also a zone of conflict. Within Bush House, as everywhere its broadcasts reach, colonial, postcolonial and Cold War conflicts clash and collude, and cosmopolitan and national imaginaries collide. Bush House exemplifies these transcultural processes beautifully. The "Tuning In" project website (see note 2) has many articles, often co-authored with BBC World Service staff, that may interest the reader.

The BBC World Service and The Open University have engaged in this unique research over nearly a decade. We offer this timely celebration of the paradoxical status of Bush House as a "home from home" for writers and broadcasters, nurturing their individual creative voices, while also producing the detached, impartial voice that has long been synonymous with the BBC. This work is also a tribute to studio managers and technical staff on whom writers and broadcasters depend. The possibilities for technical mishaps at Bush House are, of course, legion. Working with technology (as with animals and children) can often have hilarious consequences. Many of the laugh-out-loud tales here involve slapstick humour and are precipitated by accidents and errors inherent in the co-dependency of technical and journalistic staff: people running up and down the stairs and crashing into each other with spools of tape, broadcasters falling asleep at the microphone or being on air when they thought they weren't. But these are more than generic bloomer tales. Bush House is attributed with a special character and personality. Many speak of it as not just a working place: an inspirational space. In its labyrinthine corridors, polyglot people from all over the world, of highly diverse political persuasions, work side by side, sharing the same studios, though not always on the same wavelengths.

Bush House is an imposing building, part of a grandiose 1920s concrete island, a complex situated in the semi-circular space between the Strand and Aldwych: once the nexus of imperial London, enjoying panoptic vistas onto Westminster and the square mile of the City. Two large male statues, symbolising Anglo-American friendship, stand over an enormously grand portico etched, ironically, with the words "Dedicated to the Friendship of English Speaking Peoples". The grandeur of the exterior and the magnificent entrance with marble-clad walls and stairs that have hosted and impressed many a visiting dignitary from around the world (a major theme in the collection) soon vanishes as one penetrates the building that is akin to a maze or a rabbit warren – never designed to be a broadcasting organisation. Bush folklore suggests that it takes at least two years to find one's way around its four blocks. I still haven't. This contradiction between the exterior grandeur and interior chaos has symbolic and almost spiritual resonances for some staff.

The building was funded by an American, Irving T Bush, and built during the 1920s and 1930s as a trade centre. Before completion it was let for government offices and later occupied by the Inland Revenue. The official opening ceremony was performed by Lord Balfour in 1925, after which the building housed diverse companies, from Parker Pen to a Russian bookshop to what was probably the first cafeteria in London. Bush House was also home to the Z Organisation, an intelligence gathering service. There are many tales of Bush House's association with the intelligence services and some still believe that the building is full of journalist spooks. The European Service – then referred to by government ministers as the "Black Hole of Tooting Bec", the wartime code for the BBC – moved into Bush House in 1941. In the years that followed, the entire Foreign Language Services moved in and by the end of the war 44 languages were being broadcast from Bush House. The BBC has always rented Bush House, while its owners have included a Japanese pension fund, the Church in Wales and the Post Office.

The fragmented and dispersed architectural space meant that the language services often worked in isolation – some refer to this as the silo effect. The World Service long remained a very centralised organisation where the centre of gravity and power remained with the English-language news desk. Most of the language services, for some time, were seen as no more than translation factories, especially those that were not well resourced because of their lack of strategic importance to the funders, the Foreign and Commonwealth Office. Translating centrally produced news in English with a consistent editorial line meant that some services lacked autonomy and creative potential in their work, and the excess of intellectual and emotional energy often spilled over into creative writing. The under-resourced services existed in cramped conditions – often airless rooms no more than the size of a cupboard. Some worked shoulder to shoulder with people who, in their home countries, might be regarded as enemies. For example, the Tamil and Sinhalese Services occupied one small room with staff facing each other. Different South Asian services, too, worked in very close physical proximity with each other at times when politically they might have been very distant. Such relations were replicated across many of the services. But the ethos of impartial journalism meant that you left your political opinions at home – or at least they did not enter into one's journalism.

Bush House was not just a workplace to its staff – it was also a social club and, some joke, a marriage bureau. The conviviality of long night shifts and the legendary BBC Club spurred both creative and procreative capacities. Apparently, not long after a very large fish tank was installed across the entire wall of the club, the glass broke and the huge variety of colourful fish that it contained were catapulted across the bar as staff were enjoying their drinks. It was said that there was a fish for every language spoken in the world and that each fish found its compatriot. Across all the anecdotes, tales and testimonies gathered in this collection, it is apparent that it is the interstitial informal spaces (the canteen, the club, the stairways, the corridors, the lifts) that are constantly emphasised as the main contact zones – the crucial spaces of encounter, interaction, exchange and creativity. Some tales are nostalgic for a bygone era, before the 1990s when BBC director general John Birt's "Producer Choice" initiative was introduced and before "value for money" became a key criterion for funding programmes. The book shows how the best of plans and projects were cooked in these informal spaces.

Bush House and its staff have experienced constant change in adapting to shifting British geopolitical and strategic interests, as well as to new technologies and management mantras. Some of the tales beautifully capture the fraught and often comic relationship between broadcasting and technology. With the advent of computers, face-to-face interaction diminished along with the old ways of working. The "new blood policy" was implemented to refresh regularly language services. For some this meant short term contracts and job insecurity. Language staff were rarely paid at the same rate as their British managers or their domestic BBC peers. There was a fear that overseas employees might become frozen in time – that their language and idiom might become outdated and that this might interfere with the close ties forged with audiences. Some tales reflect the challenges of adjusting to changing circumstances – technological, political, cultural and linguistic – over the decades. First computers and now social media are at the forefront of policy and strategy, and once more staff will have to learn new skills, or be replaced (or at worst, both). Some of the Bush tales are nostalgic for a distant Golden Age, some are enchanting, while others have a moral import, particularly those that relate to the trials of reporting the truth in situations where personal politics and professional imperatives seem to be at odds – or, indeed, the impossibility of reporting the truth when the corroborative evidence required by the BBC was suppressed or destroyed. Some tales take the form of straight reportage, offering a recital of events or happenings, revealing not just working lives but the often controversial relationship that language services have had with the BBC management.

The collection is made up of diverse source materials. The responses to the email circulated by Hamid Ismailov to all his Bush House colleagues form a major part of the book. This material is therefore derived from a self-selecting sample of staff. Interviews conducted by the former managing director of the BBC World Service, Sir John Tusa, for two radio programmes produced by Anna Horsbrugh-

Porter[4] were extremely useful as they contained valuable accounts of some of Bush House veterans. Research conducted by The Open University also provided a wealth of interesting material that enabled us to include more voices and tales, especially from language services. We drew not only on the Bush Writers seminars, but on two others which furnished us with oral history material on how the South Asian services reported the birth of Bangladesh in 1971 (co-organised with William Crawley), and on the 70th anniversary of the Urdu Service (co-organised with David Page). All these materials are available on the project website (see note 2).

In selecting from the material available, we were mostly guided by the relevance of the tales – especially those that offered insights into Bush House culture – and by their entertainment value. Another principle was to select stories that would be representative of Bush House across time. We tried not to overlook anything of interest, however narrow, nor to overdo any particular theme. Many tales were edited – judiciously, we hope. We were also concerned to represent the greatest possible plurality of voices, languages and experiences. We had copious tales about technical mishaps in Bush House studios. We could only include some of them in the interests of balancing material. As ever, the absences strike the editors perhaps more than the content. There are many voices from the past and present that are not included for various reasons.

The content was split into chapters arranged thematically. "On Air" includes stories of the pressures and hilarity of making live continuity programmes, usually told by studio managers and others involved in their production. "Off Air" is dedicated to aspects of work and daily life in Bush House, such as curious incidents and unusual events happening outside recording studios. "History Live" contains tales that focus on the role of the BBC in world affairs – sometimes involving monumental events, at other times small but still important occasions. "Rubbing Shoulders" was initially envisaged as a chapter on visiting dignitaries, but it seemed to us to be more in the democratic spirit of the book to combine all visitors to Bush House under the same heading. "Tower of Babel" is a series of snapshots indicating what a rich environment Bush House has always been, with its mixture of languages and cultures. The title suggests a cacophony of voices failing to communicate with each other which, as the book reveals, is not quite accurate. Yet, as this is the term used in Bush folklore, we decided to keep it.

The topics of these chapters often overlap, and there are several general themes that run through the whole collection. The creative vitality and cosmopolitan spirit of Bush House, the professionalism of the BBC staff, the popularity of various World Service presenters and programmes around the world are predominant. One of the most common and endearing motifs is the tendency of the book's

4. See http://www.bbc.co.uk/programmes/p00m98kf and http://www.bbc.co.uk/programmes/p00mgpnl (accessed 30 May 2012).

contributors to remember their work at the BBC with a great sense of humour. The book's value owes a lot to the wonderful comic imagination of the contributors as they work under tight deadlines and seemingly insurmountable constraints. The collected stories vary from love letters to Bush House to critical tales and, read together, portray the World Service in all its cultural complexity. The cosmopolitan atmosphere of Bush House and struggles in the quest for truth are among the most important themes that emerge across numerous tales.

The variety of the tales collected here made our job as editors exciting and challenging. The book can be read as an integral whole or as episodic narratives. But most of all we hope that we have captured something of the cultural spirit of Bush House and that readers will smile, laugh and remember it, as we do, with affection.

Marie Gillespie

Chapter One

On Air: "Good Thing It Isn't TV"

No Niceties

One afternoon a person claiming to be a Nigerian general called Bush House demanding to be put live onto the next edition of Focus on Africa. I took the call.

"I am General A. I have to be interviewed by Mr Robin White." I replied that the programme was about to go on air. "I know at what time the programme goes on air. There will be news and then Focus will be on and I must be interviewed first on it."

When the call was re-routed through to the studio, Robin immediately said they would move everything down the order to start with the general. He did this and the general was first on.

"Robin White, is that Mr Robin White?"
"Yes, it is. What can we do for you?"
"I am General A of the Nigerian Army First Corp and we have just arrived in Sierra Leone to assist the world governments in liberating that country. I am now addressing you and your listeners through our mobile satellite phone. Robin, this is a historic day for…"
"General, can I just check this? You have arrived in Sierra Leone to bring democracy to the country?"
"Precisely. We have. We have, Robin. And now I wish to read out on behalf of the people of Nigeria…"
"Hang on, General, please. So you are bringing democracy to Sierra Leone."
"That's it. We are, Robin, we are."
"And when you go home to Nigeria, General, will you be taking democracy back there too?"

There was a wonderful wavering silence on the airwaves. At the time Nigeria was being run by Sani Abacha, brutal even by their military government's standards, who would certainly be listening to this interview and waiting for his general to respond. Still nothing from the general.

"Now Robin, Robin White, that it a nasty and most unseemly question. I will now read the proclamation..."
"No, General. You will have a chance to explain what you are doing in Sierra Leone. But could I ask again, does this mean that democracy is now breaking out in Nigeria?"

It was all live. Robin had no niceties on air; he did not need to be liked by his interviewees, he had no time for blandishments. He was never rude but absolutely nerveless.

After a bit more spluttering and dissimulating, the general's voice faded and his troops pulled the plug from his satellite phone. President Sani Abacha was later to die of a heart attack while in bed with two French prostitutes. But for now he would be eagerly waiting for the general's return.

Barry Langridge

The Mutter Box

One of the things that irritated me enormously when I was dealing with correspondents was that the quality of lines was very poor and I knew there must be some way to improve this. I got talking to another Australian, who was employed by a commercial radio station over here, and he told me he had been working on a device but wasn't sure what to do next. We got together and came up with something which was called – first jokingly, then officially – a "mutter box"; it was the size of two cassette cartridge boxes, one on top of the other.

And we were – I suspect, illegally – demolishing telephones and connecting these things straight into the line. The difference was phenomenal. It transformed our coverage because suddenly we could hear the correspondent. We could even hear Mark Tully in Delhi, which was an achievement, because the lines from India were notorious then. So it was great, but of course now it's an old hat. As I watch the news on TV and hear it on radio, I think, what amazing equipment they've got these days. The correspondents used to come around to my home. One of the bedrooms was a simulated hotel room, like those most of them had to work from, and I would show them how to get into a telephone and connect this mutter box, which was a terrific amplifier. So a correspondent would come back from the field and, once they had a telephone line back to London, they just connected this equipment up by crocodile clips to the inside of the telephone – it was a very, very simple device. They could plug. They could set, record us or use old reel-to-reel machines and just transmit; it opened the world for us.

You might get away with a relatively poor sound in domestic broadcasting with medium wavelength and FM, but with short-wave radio you had to always go for the maximum quality, and that's what the mutter box did.

Ian Richardson

The Wrong Programme

When we went to transition from tape to digital I was doing World Business, a business report that went out in the evening. For some reason I decided to edit the programme on tape rather than using this newfangled digital technology. I don't really know why – I suppose it was just force of habit.

That programme was recorded very close to transmission because it was a business report. We had to be up to date and for some reason we were running very late. So I had to put the first half of the programme on air before I had finished editing the whole thing, slicing it in two. I knew the first half was OK.

Having stuck it on air, I carried on editing the other half of the programme. I was madly working away with my razor blade and my chinagraph pencil, when the presenter tapped me on the shoulder and said, "Giles, old boy." "Not now, a bit busy." "Giles, I really need to talk to you." "Bit up against it. Sorry, can I just get on with editing this?" Then he said, "This is the wrong programme." I had accidentally picked up the wrong spool of tape from the back of the studio and put it on air. So I was actually broadcasting a business report from several days previously and I'd like to think I caused a small run on the yen that night.

Giles Booth

The Cough Key

John Tusa once decided that he would find out what went on during night shifts and wandered around Bush House in the course of the night. The managing director was coming to watch the night shifts, so we were all terribly excited about it and impressed with his commitment, but he did seem to jinx the place that time.

We were preparing for the Latin American transmission which went out at about 1:15am, for four hours. Quite a busy programme, a lot of tapes and news bulletins and things to cope with – and then Tusa came along. After a quick line-up we were all ready to go, I made a last check of the microphones just to make sure they were working, but they were silent. As it turned out, the so-called cough key in the studio had got stuck. So the microphones were muted.

We had no option but to use what was basically a little musical jingle that went out constantly to sustain the frequency and to keep the transmission on air. In the meantime, we had to ring the duty manager and say, "Have you got another studio that we can run to?" He found one, so we gathered all the tapes up in our arms and the whole team ran to the next studio – within about eight or 10 minutes we were back on the air. John Tusa wrote it up in a short diary piece in the *Sunday Times* that week: at last, my name in the papers!

Jonathan Kempster

Keeping Transmitters on

The demands of domestic news, and in some respects the increasing parochialism of domestic news, leads in one direction and then the World Service has to have its own world agenda. It's always been thus. That was why I wanted to have the World Service English broadcast on a domestic frequency, or least one which was audible in the UK. You'd be surprised how many people have said, "Well, I don't think it should be heard in the UK because, after all, British voters don't pay for it." But we said, "Well, you'd be amazed how many of the UK audience want to hear it." We used to be on long wave for a while, a couple of hours after Radio 4 shut down, before it opened up again. And then one day, an engineer said to me, "Would you like to have the World Service on all through the night?" "Yes, but how much would it cost?" "Well, I don't think it would cost anything." So I asked, "Really, why?" And he said, "Well, a lot of the time, the transmitters have cooled down and by the time you've powered them up, you might as well leave them running the whole time." This was completely untrue, of course, but they just thought it was stupid not to have it available to UK listeners. So there were all sorts of wonderfully collusive people in the BBC.

John Tusa

Click Click

Ron Farrow, a really uplifting fellow, told this tale better than I can. An announcer in a self-op studio with one of those very large slowly rotating discs with an English by Radio programme on it, completed the introductory announcement and, as he sped out of the studio for the BBC Club in Surrey Street, across the road from Bush, he started the disc, as well as his stopwatch. He came back just in time for the predicted end of the programme – only to hear something like "Hello listeners, and welcome t... (click) ... Hello listeners, and welcome t... (click) ... Hello listeners, and welcome t..."

David Carlsen

Playing at Half Speed

Whenever there was a big story breaking you would physically shake. For example, back in the 1980s, the Polish service used to have 19 million listeners and it was all down to little old me, sitting in front of this rather old-fashioned 1950s mixing desk, producing the whole transmission and making everything go well. Surprisingly few mistakes were made, but the night shift was when they were made. At four o'clock in the morning you are at your lowest.

My worst mistake was on the English stream at about two o'clock in the morning as I was playing out a tape. In those days we used to borrow quite a lot of material from Broadcasting House and their tapes ran at a different speed from ours. Bush

House tapes ran at 7.5 inches per second and at Broadcasting House it was 15 inches per second.

The protocol was that you would monitor the first minute of a tape and then line it up ready for playing out when the continuity announcer queued you. So I listen to this tape. Listened to the first minute – it started with some strange music, but music nonetheless. I rounded back, queued it up, waited for the announcer to read the intro. After I played it in, we sat there for a minute or so and then we realised that it was a Broadcasting House tape – playing at half-speed.

Jonathan Kempster

Quality Control

When the former Soviet Union turned at last from communism and went falteringly towards capitalism, the BBC World Service thought it could help. It would co-produce a number of attractive programmes illustrating the problems of the change, and how some of these might be surmounted. There were short snappy series, there was a soap opera scripted by Russians but led by a writer from The Archers and set in an apartment block where one or two people were trying to develop businesses, and so on.

One set of programmes would be fly-on-the wall documentaries about a real-life factory entering the consumer market. An expert would help. We went to the factory and were welcomed. It had been building shell cases. Now it had moved to microwaves – which did look very like shell cases. No one would buy, the managers maintained, because everybody who could afford such goods wanted foreign-built stuff since Russian equipment was thought of as low-grade and unreliable.

The expert decided to dedicate two days to quality control. By the afternoon of the second day he told us that even the brightest sparks from the factory just couldn't get their heads round the concept. We recorded the ensuing lesson.

Expert: "So now we know what a brand is. And you build a brand around reputation, and you build reputation by reliability and low cost, and you establish that by quality control." There was a pause while this was translated. Expert (picking out the youngest manager): "For example, Pyotr, let's say I am making radios, and I sell you one, and when you take it home it doesn't work. What would you do?" Pyotr (after hearing the translation): "What would I do? I would sell it." Expert, suddenly a little tired: "Let's leave it there for now."

Barry Langridge

Webmadams

In 1993 an American cousin came over from California for a week. He stayed with our aunt, and perplexed her by unplugging her phone and sticking a wire from his laptop into the socket. I think she felt it was rather disrespectful to the phone. John showed me the new world of the Internet, page after page of dark grey text on a slightly less dark grey background. It looked like a fun place to teach English. Chris Westcott became the first World Service — what to call him — "Webmaster", it said on the door of his office. Karen Chilton came to work with him on the new World Service website, joined later by Sally Thompson. After a bit of thought their door proudly sported the sign "Webmadams".

BBC English had moved down from Queens House back to Bush and became one of the first departments to go on a network. (Grumbles were heard throughout Bush: "Just give me one good reason why I should want to let anyone else see my documents.") I worked with Katie Elvin (now Barrett) and we launched the BBC English website at a teachers' conference in March 1996. Katie was soon accorded the crucial right to transfer material to the site directly, and Karen helped us get a virtual summer school running that August. A recording — nobody was worrying about rights back then — of a barn dance was our first audio file. Learners could download the two minute clip in — oh, anything under 30 minutes.

Our students could communicate with us by email. Nothing really new there (in the olden days listeners managed it quite well by means of a letter in an envelope — remember them?); programmes based on English language questions sent in by listeners had been going since 1947. Now, however, learners could, in theory, communicate not just with us but with each other, through discussion lists. Except that they couldn't, owing to an apparently insoluble problem caused by incompatible email systems. The problem was solved one day when Karen talked to Brandon Butterworth, who was on a visit to Bush. "Sure, I can fix it," he said.

Our procession across the canteen floor up to the North East wing made me think (rather fancifully) of druids: Brandon, the high priest of the New Way, followed by Karen, bearing not mistletoe but a Microsoft manual, with Katie and I following on as acolytes.

We tried our first major live webcast at an English language teaching conference in Edinburgh in 1999. In the hall Paul Scott was producing the debate. The presenter was David Thomas, managing editor of the BBC English Production (no point in having a fancy title like that if you can't have some fun). Outside, clutching my laptop, hooked up to a dodgy connection, I heard the applause of the audience – from inside the hall. Then came muffled voices – from inside the hall. David Thomas, who was used to the immediacy of radio, introduced the panellists. "Welcome to this BBC English debate from Edinburgh…" Still silence out in the corridor. Wrong sort of ISDN line? Over-optimistic idea in the first place? An eternity of buffering. Finally, a tinny sound from the laptop, far worse quality than any jammed short-wave transmission on its third hop: "Welcome to this BBC English debate from Edinburgh…"

Hamish Norbrook

ABCDN

Malcolm Eynon, who later became a continuity announcer for the World Service and BBC TV, was a good friend of mine on our studio manager course in 1972. At Bush House we set off on the dreadful shift system prevalent at that time, known as ABCDN, starting with a late afternoon shift, getting earlier through the week and then culminating with a night shift. The three days off after that were richly deserved! But the working week was eight days rather than seven, so our social and family lives were thrown into chaos – as were my stomach and brain. In the late 1980s I was lucky enough to get promoted and never did another night. Back in those early days, Malcolm and I were on the same 'clump', a group that did the same shifts regularly, so he and I were together during one of our long and rather boring night shifts. At that time studio managers had to make opening announcements on cubicle microphones to open a certain transmission.

At about 04:30, on one of these occasions in early 1973, I was alone in studio S4 on the ground floor of the South East wing in Bush. I was about to make an announcement for an English By Radio programme – it had been completely pre-recorded, so I had no one on the other side of the glass; it would have been a programme with enough play-out music at the end for me to fade out.

As I sat at a control panel, at 29 minutes and 30 seconds past four o'clock in the morning, trying to stay alert and looking vaguely into the darkened studio through the insulated glass, I reached to turn on the cubicle mic and say the immortal words "This is BBC English By Radio broadcasting to Europe, etc." when, on the other side of the window, coming up into my view rose a very large piece of paper, and on it, in huge black lettering were the words: "FART NOW". Thanks, Malcolm!

Dave Johnstone

Tears on Air

When an Arabic Service journalist, Mohamed Mustafa Ramadan, was murdered outside Regent's Park mosque after a Friday prayer on the 11th of April 1980, I was just beginning my shift as a reader. As the news came, I took the whole thing and I went upstairs. The newsroom was on the fourth floor in Bush House and the studio was on the seventh floor.

So I took the whole bunch of news, not realizing what was happening really, till I opened the microphone and started to read the news of Mohamed Mustafa Ramadan being killed or murdered. At this, I started crying and couldn't finish. They were listening to me from downstairs. Somebody came straight up to the seventh floor, took over from me and I just left the studio, still crying. Then I came back but not to read the news, just to do the continuity.

A Saudi friend asked, "Why did you cry on air?" "It was a murder, it was shocking." He said, "Somebody would think that you were in love with him." But he was a colleague, I knew him and I knew his daughter, who usually went with him to every Friday prayer. This time, luckily for her, she went with her mother to the ladies' section, so didn't witness the shooting of her father. As all these pictures came to my mind when I was reading the news, I couldn't control my emotions – I cried on air.

Huda Al-Rasheed

Slapstick Live

I was doing a programme late at night and there was just me and the presenter. He seemed to be having trouble reading as he kept coughing. I was wondering why he didn't use the cough button when I noticed it was on the other table, beyond his reach. So while he continued to read, I crept into the studio and moved it to his table; he nodded appreciatively. Turning to leave the studio, I tripped over the cable and fell flat on my face. The presenter burst out laughing on air.

Colin Neal

In Timely Fashion

I remember working with Freddie Payne, a newsreader who had the ability to catnap during the news – always waking up in time to read the next item.

Caroline Dunton

No-Show

Another funny story happened at the time when there had to be identifying opening announcements made in English, and the studio manager who was supposed to be covering this programme at about 4:30 had not shown up. The presenter rang the director, with a couple of minutes to go. He was tucked up in his little bed, in the corner of the office upstairs, but of course leapt into action, rushed downstairs in his pyjamas, clutching the spare layout, to save the day. As he held the cubicle mic fader in one hand and the layout in the other, the cord on his pyjama bottoms came untied. Trooper that he was, he continued his announcement and proceeded to open the mic for the presenter to begin reading the news. This, unfortunately, the presenter was unable to do for some seconds, being convulsed with laughter.

Lynne Plummer

15 Minutes of Snoring

A Czech service producer was working alone on a night shift; he went in the studio, prepared the material and dozed off! As he left the mike open, Czech listeners had a pleasure to listen to 15 minutes of his snoring – live on air!

Zaneta Skerlev

Studio Boredom

Some of the very long vernacular transmissions – as the foreign language services were known at Bush – broadcast by the Russians and the Poles, for instance, included pre-recorded sections that were nearly half an hour long, and this inevitably led to boredom in the studios. Russian presenters would sometimes amuse themselves by playing chess on air, and their colleagues in the cubicle would try and catch them out. This involved getting the studio manager to cut the studio speaker suddenly and flash the green light, whilst waving urgently, as if the tape had unexpectedly come to an end, and the presenters were required to fill in immediately. The trick couldn't be repeated too often.

Boredom was more of a problem for the studio managers, because not only were the tapes long, they were also in a foreign language, so listening was tedious. This meant that people weren't always concentrating one hundred percent; there was a tendency to dim the loudspeaker and get a newspaper out (or knitting, or whatever), and there were countless occasions when the tape came to an end while the studio manager was quietly nodding off, especially on night shifts.

One very senior studio manager once decided, during a long tape, to nip back to the common room and pick up his coat, so he could make a quick getaway at the end of the transmission. On his way back to the studio, he bumped into a friend who was on his way home, got talking, and before he knew it, the two of them were deep in conversation on a bus in the Strand! The studio manager always claimed that he remembered in time, leapt off the bus and got back to the cubicle just in time to see the tape coming to an end.

Pete Rawlings

Reverse Order

During an hour-long Latin American Spanish transmission, it was very important not to make any mistakes because this programme was recorded and re-broadcast later in the night. They had two studio managers working on it, one who mixed the sound and another who was playing tapes. I was doing that one night. They brought the material to the studio on a big spool of reel tape rather than bringing lots of little ones because there would have been far too many for an hour.

It was a 2,400-foot reel tape, a massive spool about the size of an old LP if anyone remembers what they were like. And we went on air. The programme started and the presenter queued in the first clip of sound to be played. When I played it everyone started to shake their heads and wave madly. I thought I must have made a mistake, so I shut the feeder.

I spooled the tape through the next band lined up and played the next tape; the same thing happened again. Everybody was waving madly and just articulating through the glass at me. I carried on and played the third band; the same thing happened again, so in the end we had to abandon the whole transmission. I think we just played music and the whole programme had to be remade later.

And it turned out, the lady who had prepared the tape for the evening transmission was new and she had made the tape up in reverse order. There were probably 30 or 40 inserts on this tape, so we could have been there the whole night before we realised actually what had happened.

Giles Booth

Down the Stairwell

In the days when programmes were recorded on shellac discs a producer left his eighth floor Centre Block office to go to a studio with a stack of pre-recorded items on a disc, tripped up on the stairs, sent the whole lot crashing down the stairwell to the basement. Everyone had to be pulled out of the BBC Club to do the programme live. You can imagine what it sounded like.

Hugh Saxby

"There's Really no Need to Take That Tone With Me, Mr Brown"

Two groups of staff at Bush House who were crucial to the success of live programmes were the studio managers and the telephonists.

Studio managers could make or break a programme, and often had to use their own judgement when an incompetent or new producer dithered over decisions on air. Young producers had to come to the studio early, with a clearly set-out plan of action – but also to be prepared for last-minute changes of the plan as the news changed. Most producers hadn't got a clue about the potential or limitations of Bush House's old studios – indeed some youngsters struggled even to locate the right studio in its labyrinth. Many of us have nightmares, even now, of running down endless corridors as the clocks are ticking down. It was soon made clear to novices that with live programmes to all parts of the world and with live lines to correspondents, 'It'll be all right on the night' was not a wise approach.

When news broke and it was necessary for the producer to change the running order, drop items and open a live line to Cairo or Beijing, it was often up to the studio manager, aided by the presenter of the programme, to effect these changes smoothly and to sail across the rough water while the producer was left as a virtual spectator.

For years, being a studio manager could be a dull task. But as competition rose and young managers demanded livelier stuff, the role of a studio manager grew in stature, and when the number of overseas bureaux doubled and trebled, we travelled regularly to train staff, or were even seconded for long periods, to the advantage of live two-ways, discussions, features and so on.

However, technical experts could sometimes do little when a bumbling producer was on a shift. Here it is important to recall the crucial role of Bush telephonists. They were hidden in the depths of Bush House, unseen to all, but they held a trove of knowledge. You wanted the correspondent in Dushanbe, live? They would get her for you. Rome, Beijing, Rio, no problem. Even when they were given little or no notice, they could cope. Often they knew the correspondent by name and would help keep them on hold before switching them through to the live studio – so the link to the live presenter was constant.

Yet a bumbler could bring everything down. One producer, a clever historian who got nervous in a live studio and always had his scripts written out hours before time, did bring everyone down one evening. His programme was running as pre-plotted –

the news, the latest from the Middle East, John Tusa in the presenter's chair, all would be well. But then as the programme began, the telephone light in the studio cubicle went on. It was a reporter in Bangkok – it might have been Al Dawson – saying that he was witnessing from his hotel window a horrible scene of the police firing on students in the street below. His line was difficult, so could we please phone him back immediately.

If the producer had kept calm and moved swiftly, there was plenty of time to drop items and get Dawson on live, and of course John would handle it beautifully. But Mr Brown did not keep his cool, and the following scene ensued.

Brown to telephonist: "Quick, quick, get Dawson, he's in Bangkok!"
Telephonist: "Right, Mr Brown, so this is Mr Al Dawson in Bangkok?"
Brown: "Yes, yes, don't dawdle, get him, get him now!"
Telephonist: "There's no need to shout, Mr Brown."
Tusa to the world (very smoothly): "Now we are getting reports from Bangkok of riots and police action against students. We are hoping to have our colleague Al Dawson live."
Brown to the world (lurches past the studio manager, presses the wrong keys): " Getting Dawson now if the bloody telephonist..."
Dawson: "Hello, hello, John, can you hear me?"
Tusa: "Al, yes, we can hear you. Could you describe exactly what you are seeing, right now?"
Telephonist to the world: "Mr Dawson is through to you now, Mr Brown."
Brown to the world, including Al Dawson and Tusa: "I know he is! I know he is! Oh, get off the line, you silly woman!"
Dawson: "What, what? John?"
Tusa: "Go ahead, Al. Al Dawson from Bangkok live. Now what..."
Telephonist to all: "There's really no need to take that tone with me, Mr Brown."
Brown to all (knuckles jammed onto the wrong keys): "Get off! Shut up, get away!"
Dawson: "John, John, are you still there?"
Tusa (makes swiping motions towards the cubicle and towards Brown): "Sorry, Al, a little technical difficulty here. Now what..."
Telephonist, again to the world: "We're just trying to do our job, Mr Brown."

The studio manager at last prises Brown away from the keys; an editor barges through the door and hustles Brown out; Dawson and Tusa deliver the goods; the studio manager handles the rest of the programme. Brown is asked to leave the building immediately but not before going down to the telephonists and begging their pardons. The telephonists do not accept his apology and are going to write a letter. Their goodwill is precious, indeed, vital. The editor goes down and begs their forgiveness on his knees. Brown is never seen or heard on live radio again. Ever. He is sent away to his doom – into the bottomless pit of Special Projects.

Barry Langridge

Pranksters

To enliven the five-hour-long night time live broadcast to Spanish-speaking America, presenters used to play practical jokes on each other. This might involve cutting the newsreader's tie in half whilst they were reading the news. On another occasion the co-presenter would tie the newsreader's shoelaces together or wear joke glasses with bouncy eyeballs popping out. A pet hamster was let loose in the studio to sniff around the cue lights or eat peanuts out of the ashtray (you could smoke in those days). Success would only be achieved if there was no discernible audible impact on the transmission.

Hugh Saxby

Good Thing It Isn't TV!

In the early 1970s the BBC World Service broadcast in English and some 40 other languages, covering the main listening times area by area. Only the English Service broadcast throughout 24 hours. The World Service continuity announcer's job was to stitch together often mutually incompatible programmes, by filling in under-runs and by advising listeners on the most effective short-wave frequencies in their area. They also announced forthcoming broadcasts likely to be of interest to the audience at that time. Not a great deal of scope for creativity!

On one occasion I was attempting to bridge a totally unexpected under-run of a previous programme, totally unaware of the frantic signals from the continuity engineer in the control cubicle on the other side of the sound-proof glass.
After the chimes of Big Ben, heard throughout the world, I duly carried on my formal introduction to an edition of Great Recordings followed by... silence. The truth was

that the half-hour pre-recorded tape was still in the Recorded Programmes Library, five floors below us in the Centre Block.

It so happened that the new engineer-in-charge was being shown round the continuity studio by my boss at the time – red faces all round. In an attempt to help us out of our mutual embarrassment, my boss came to the help of his troop by cueing-up a music disc on the studio turntable – but at the wrong speed, and with an impressive hiss of surface noise before the music began ("here is part of a gramophone record").

There was always an hysterical side to broadcasting – like giggling in church. Good thing it isn't TV.

Terry Jarvis

Fatchy Pog

It's the middle of the night and in my new role as a studio manager I'm manning the Green Room where the BBC World Service announcers read news bulletins to the great and the good throughout the world. Unfortunately, they're not always in peak condition when they arrive. I've already witnessed one announcer saying "BBC World Service. It's 11 hours Greenwich Mean Time and I'm..." and then being completely unable to remember his own name. Another announcer, describing the weather in England, said there was "fatchy pog" all over London.

This evening my newsreader, Jerry, comes crashing into the studio, ten minutes late. "Do youssh want shummm level then?" Good Lord, I think. This man is completely out of it. In one minute 27 seconds he's going to be live on air with the world news and he's as drunk as a newt. There's really nothing I can do, short of marching into the studio and reading the news myself. "Yes – let's have some level," I say. "BBCsh Worldshh SHERVice mmmd ffghod..." says Jerrry, and burps loudly. "You've got 27 seconds to sober up," I announce primly.

The second hand ticks on relentlessly. The announcer is now slouched in his seat, dozing. I wonder if my BBC career is going to come to a very short, undignified end. I'm bound to be tainted by association with the forthcoming disaster. "Wake up!" I hiss, over the talkback. "Five seconds!" I give him a green light. For a moment there's complete silence. Then — miracle of miracles — I hear a deep breath and, slightly slower than usual, but without a single slur or hesitation: "BBC World Service. Here is the news from London. It has been announced from Washington that..." and so on, and so forth, for exactly nine minutes, until we hear the magic words: "And that is the end of the news from London." At which point very slowly, and with great dignity, Jerry leans back in his chair, and slides, unconscious, to the floor.

Gordon House

Mic off

A sports producer is dispatched halfway across the world to cover the Brisbane Commonwealth Games for the African services. At each sporting event he locates the nearest microphone and delivers his piece at the appointed time. After a few days he gets a phone call. "Are you OK? It's just that we haven't heard from you." It turned out that he harboured the false assumption that all broadcast technology always worked perfectly. He assumed that all microphones at official venues were switched through at the booked time to the destination (i.e., the Bush House studio).

Hugh Saxby

Very Warm Welcome

The spring of 2010 saw the end of live continuity. I was on that last day and I felt anxious to let the listeners know that we were broadcasting live. Normally, with continuity, you would not really know it was live. It happened to be the warmest day in London so far that year, so I had time to say, "Here in London it's the warmest day of the year so far – 72 degrees Fahrenheit, 22 degrees Celsius, so if you have just joined us, a very WARM welcome to the BBC World Service!"

Jonathan Wheatley

Yesterday's News

When I joined the BBC, Bush House was under threat from financial cuts. Nothing new there. I had just started as a studio manager – a wonderful job which was all about helping producers to broadcast their programmes. Usually this meant following a well-organised script but occasionally it meant rescuing hapless broadcasters from chaos of their own making, often the most satisfying part.

Listeners to the External Services (as it was then called) in the early 1980s would have been largely oblivious to these occasional behind-the-scenes dramas. So it was that during a night shift I sat down to read my newspaper as I waited for a German newsreader to arrive in the studio. Normally one wouldn't get alarmed until about three minutes to go. Then the lady turned up, a little flustered – it was her first week as a producer. She proceeded into the studio having given me her pre-recorded press review tape which would be needed after the news.

Everything seemed normal as the red light came on and the opening sequence ran its usual course. Then our newbie broadcaster started to read the news, which was continuous speech in those days. After about five minutes of her allotted nine I noticed a number of long pauses and shuffling of papers. Recovering my senses (it was about 5am) I could see she was really agitated so I asked (in her headphones) what the problem was. She pressed the cough button which cut off the broadcast sound and said to me: "I'm reading yesterday's news... not today's... what do I do?" Mmmmm, a tricky one. "End the news and play the press review. Can you get to the office and grab today's headlines and get back in four minutes 30 seconds, when the press review ends?" She made it with seconds to spare and read the correct morning's headlines in a somewhat breathless style – she translated and read them live. Then to fill for time she read them again. "Oh no, I will lose my job," she said in a panic afterwards.

The next week I saw her again – she was smiling. It appeared that nobody had noticed and I'm pleased to say that the lady in question went on to become a highly respected journalist and broadcaster until the German Service closed in 1999.

Hugh Saxby

A Flying Change

I still remember the shock I had at Bush House when the elevator refused service and I had to rush seven floors down the stairs to read the news. Out of breath, I was there just in time, got through half a minute and would have died if it hadn't been for the luck that a colleague was in the cubicle to take over in a flying change. And in hindsight, it was not about life and death. It was only the rigour of discipline and performance which, thank you, Beeb, helped many of us go further in our careers.

Merve Hoelter

Reading Red Lights

It had been another long day in Arabic continuity (a "continuity" is the studio that links all the other programmes recorded or live from other studios). It was half past seven in the evening, just half an hour before the transmission ended. The newsreader for the final 20 minutes turned up with his thick script and sat down at his desk from where he would also close the programme. It was just a desk with a microphone and a switch which turned the microphone on and off together with the red light of the continuity studio. The Arabic newsreader was newish to the job and would just have received his training, where he would have been told that a normal studio was live on air when the red light was on. I don't think he had done a daytime Arabic transmission before. Anyway, the continuity announcer finished the back announcement for the last recorded programme and introduced the Arabic newsreader. That was the end of the shift for the announcer, who collected up all his bits and pieces and crept out of the studio and left the newsreader to finish the transmission. The newsreader got on with his task. It sounded quite smooth and unhesitant, maybe a little slow. The end of the transmission came. I put on my coat, picked up the programme box and wandered into the studio where the newsreader was. I said, "Ayoub, you can stop reading now." The minute or so since the end of the transmission, poor Ayoub had been continuing to read diligently from the carefully prepared news script, unaware that his voice was reaching our control room but no further. I think he was under the impression that because the red light was on, the continuity was live on air, whereas it was on only because he had turned his microphone switch on. Ayoub completed many successful news bulletins after that.

David Carlsen

The Birth of Arabic Online

I launched the BBC Arabic website, and the BBC Arabic radio people are incredibly grand, they wear cravats. I remember trying to get someone to have their annual appraisal done and he said, "I'm not going to have my appraisal done." "What about Mr Ahmed?" "He's from Yemen. Do you think you're ever going to find a Jordanian who will be appraised by a Yemeni?" "Well, who can you be appraised with?" "I'll be appraised by you, you're a pukka English gentleman." I said, "I don't want to! What about so-and-so?" "He's a Jordanian refugee!"

Anyway, I told that presenter, "Look, in your morning programme – it was a long rolling programme right across the hours of the Arabic community in the Middle East – we'll have the online people come over to you and you'll say to them, 'What's online today?'" The answer was, "Well, what's 'online'?" "Online is what's going to stay at the Arabic service." "Well, I'm not going to talk to these people, their Arabic is horrible!"

And then there was that awful aircraft problem with the Egyptian pilot who may or may not have committed suicide, and I went in overnight and said, "There's a graphic being put up online, showing why the man might have committed suicide, why he might not have committed suicide." I had to stand there and physically say at 25 minutes past, "Stop!" And the online guy was then interviewed by this incredibly snotty grandee, saying, "Well, what's on your little site today?" Afterwards I had him in my office and said, "I don't want to discipline you, you're too grand to be disciplined, but this 'little site' is the future of the Arabic service." This is how the first Arabic online service was born.

Barry Langridge

Anybody There?

There's the commercial way of doing things, and then there's the BBC way. I still remember a night shift about ten years ago, just after a number of self-ops in the South East wing had been fitted with new sound desks – with the faders the wrong (i.e. commercial) way round. I was working in the control room and one of the networks suddenly went very quiet – no sound coming from studio and nobody answering any phones. After a certain amount of running around it turned out that whoever had used the studio last had left the fader open, the newsreader coming in had forgotten the different faders, so when the red light came on he smartly closed the fader, read his bulletin and when the red light went off he opened the fader again. Of course, the reason he didn't answer our frantic phone calls was that he was – as he thought – on air!

Hild Myklebust

In Need of a Main Gain Bypass

It was a Swahili transmission in studio C22 when this happened. The transmission was going swimmingly as I recall. The red light was on and the news in Swahili was coming out of the speaker. While it was going on a current affairs producer came into the studio clutching his newly honed script. He put it on the script surface which ran along the length of the studio desk in front of the studio manager. Having subtly topped it off with a cup of coffee, he picked up the script again. The coffee cup tipped forward spilling all its contents on to the sound desk and, as it was not a frappuccino (they were not invented yet), it was thin enough to drain down by the side of the main fader. Everything went rather quiet – you could hear a pin drop… well, the sound of dripping coffee, anyway. Then I thought and may have said, "There's no main gain bypass!"

That very powerful image of coffee disappearing down a thin slot by the side of the main gain fader made me think I needed a main gain bypass. Like you imagine you may be in need of a heart bypass if your heart stops. No matter how hard I looked, there just wasn't one. But was the whole output of the desk dead? The newsreader's mouth on the other side of the glass was still moving but that did not mean everything was dead. I thought about putting on a tape to get some programme output on air but that didn't work. After what seemed like a lifetime and maybe a few "oh Gods", the Swahili transmission came back on the speaker and on air – just like that. Apparently, the coffee had seeped into a relay and activated it. After just over a minute gravity had pulled enough of the coffee through the relay for everything to return to normal – well, the normal insanity of Bush House, that is.

David Carlsen

Imaginary Sound

A BBC Somali presenter repeatedly apologised to listeners for the background sound of a different BBC language broadcast which he thought was drowning out his news bulletin. It turned out that the studio manager had switched the wrong ring main feed to his headphones and the background sound was entirely imaginary.

Hugh Saxby

Our Unworldly Friend

A well-connected but unworldly member of staff was asked to produce a discussion programme. He noticed that the presenter was wearing headphones. Being the producer, he felt he should also have a set. The studio manager patiently explained that the presenter needed headphones to hear instructions from the cubicle; the producer didn't need any because he could hear everything going on in the studio without them. But our unworldly friend insisted. So the studio manager found him a pair. The producer then sat proudly and happily wearing his headphones throughout the recording – unaware they weren't plugged into anything.

Ian Richardson

Bush Ghosts

I was a studio manager at Bush for seven years from 1961. There was a rumour that a ghost walked at night on the ground floor of the South East wing. I was doing the dawn chorus, as the series of back-to-back 15-minute transmissions was known to us. While a presenter was reading the news in front of me in the studio, the main door was opened and steps vibrated down the little passage beside the cubicle and towards the studio... I leapt to the cubicle door to protect my presenter, but although the footsteps were clearly audible there was nobody there. Spooky? Definitely!

Lynne Plummer

Reporting From the Battlefield

It was a bright sunny day in Bush House and we got a phone call from the EPRDF, the Ethiopian Rebel Movement. They claimed a big battle they had won in Adua or some place and I asked, "Where are you calling from?" because normally they had a spokesperson.

I think their spokesperson was from Belgium and that's where they often called us from. But this man was purporting to be reporting from the battlefield. He was giving me names of villages in northern Ethiopia, and it was a very clear line. I said, "That cannot be," but he told me he was calling from a satellite phone. I wasn't very techno-savvy and we had never received a call from a satellite phone on the programme before, so of course, we were very sceptical. I said to him, "Look outside the window and describe what you can see for me," because I thought he might be calling us from Kingsway or something like that. He replied, "What do you mean, out of the window? I am not at any window. I am right here on the field." We did broadcast it with a little trepidation, but it soon turned out that he was right.

Elizabeth Ohene

Wo King

An announcer was unable to successfully voice a piece about the advantages of lion dung over tiger dung – just couldn't stop laughing. A sports announcer was struggling to control himself when he realised the "World Table Tennis Championships in Wo King" was, in fact, taking place in Surrey, and not (as he had assumed) in China. Poor chap was almost reduced to tears as he tried to finish the bulletin.

Hugh Saxby

A Tale of Two Mice

The Hindustani service began on the 11th of May 1940. I used to come in as a casual but actually joined in 1941. We started features about the war and how things were on different fronts. This was serious creative work and we used sound effects to spice it up: for instance, pouring sand created a rain effect and vibrating metal plates was good enough for wind effects – these were all live sound effects because the features were not recorded. All live broadcasting it was. That included children's programmes where the presenter used to read a story, a story of two mice. One was a typical English mouse and the other had just arrived from India and the two would go out for sightseeing in London. He was a great storyteller and the story became very popular. It had all the right ingredients: a lot of adventure, good storyline and a good voice. The music was quite effective, too. It was Henry Purcell's *Trumpet Voluntary*, followed by the announcer's voice.

Iqbal Bahadur Sarin

Who Is the Rabbit?

When I joined the BBC there was a Pashto Service programme called The World of Youth. For it we were supposed to either translate some material about new discoveries or interview Afghans inside Afghanistan or outside. And I proposed to my editor that I could write for children – that was something I thought was lacking, something for five or six-year-olds.

And then a colleague suggested that I use a special machine which would allow me to change my voice to create a character. My character was a rabbit. I would talk to her and read a story, and then she would interrupt me, asking all sorts of silly questions, the kind of questions children usually ask. My daughter was five at that time, so I used to read my stories to her and then put her questions into the rabbit's mouth. I wrote a story about a little girl who lost her mother and she stopped washing her face and brushing her hair. Then she sees her mother in her dream and the mother says, well, I'm still there, I'm still watching you. When she wakes up and starts brushing her hair, it's a step in the right direction.

My colleague went to Kabul. He came back and he said, "Najiba, this big Taliban commander came to me and whispered in my ear, 'Who is this rabbit? Is that a little girl? How old is she?'" I had to change my accent then – that was one way to convince people that it was not me.

Najiba Kasraee

Gangster Approach

One day I was approached by my boss, Brian Matcham, who said, "Barry, we've changed your schedule a bit. Could you put the Bulgarians on air? Oh, and keep your wits about you." This I did, noting that the announcers were not quite their usual selves. On returning, I asked Brian what that was all about. "Haven't you heard: the dissident broadcaster, Georgy Markov, has been killed with a poisoned umbrella while crossing Waterloo Bridge, and there was just a chance that the Bulgarian Secret Service could invade the studio." "Why did you send me?" I asked. "Well, I've always regarded you as a bit of a gangster, and if there were any problems, you were the best one to deal with them!"

Barry Mitchell

Female Orgasm in Brown River Trout

Quite often an outside contributor would call the control room with only a vague idea as to what they should be contributing to. When somebody insists their piece is for "World Service, don'tcha know? No, can't remember the chap's name! What section? World Service, I said!" – that's when a spot of detective work is required. I will never forget the man who called in and was finally found a home with a science programme after informing us in a perfectly serious and straight voice that he was doing a piece on "female orgasm in brown river-trout." The variation in subjects covered in this building has never ceased to provide amusement and delight!

Hild Myklebust

Chapter Two

Off Air: "Look Neither Eager nor Flurried"

Dusty Secret

I worked for a time as a specialist studio manager on the seventh floor of Centre Block. Most floors in Centre Block have a corridor that goes away from the double doors leading from the central staircase in both directions. At the end of the corridor furthest away from the central staircase on the seventh floor there was a door that I passed every day. It was an interesting, maybe important sort of door, the only one in that wall. With a brass lever handle and a single large keyhole, it looked like a safe. After passing this door for at least a couple of years, I thought that the lever handle could do with a bit of a polish. Next time I passed the door not in a hurry I gave the handle a bit of a polish. It moved a bit. I put the handle back to the vertical position, listened – no alarms were going off. Next time I passed the door handle when I really wasn't in a hurry and nobody else was looking, I gave the handle a good turn and pulled the door. What did I expect to see: piles of money? cobwebs? skeletons?

On opening the door fully I faced a black hole. After quite a few seconds I could just make out a blank wall, half-blackened, in front of me! Excited, I carefully stepped across the door threshold into the gloom. To the left of me there was blackness, to the right of me the same, above me more blackness but lighter in colour. This indicated that the ceiling was closer to me than the far wall of this void. It slowly became clearer that there was something at the end of this space. Piles of money! The thought crossed my mind again. I looked back and there, beside the door was a black object. More black than the wall. It looked like a light switch. It was old but 20th century, and it worked a bulb hanging from the ceiling! A single clear bulb shone through the cobwebs surrounding it, illuminating the space to a brilliant grey colour and that stuff at the ends, some sort of printed papers coated in filthy cobwebs – so not money, after all. The ceiling wasn't horizontal. It sloped down from the middle to the piles of blackened paper at each end. I crept up to one of them and gingerly

41

took a small handful out of the filthy pile. Many copies of the same thing! I took them back to the doorway under the light and leafed through the bundle. Each page had the Royal Air Force roundel at the top. It was in French. I confirmed later that these were RAF airdrop leaflets that did not make it to occupied northern France during the Second World War.

Later a chap from French for Europe passed through one of my studios and mentioned that he was setting up an exhibition on the BBC broadcasting to France during the Second World War, so I told him about these leaflets and took him to the dust pile on the seventh floor. He was quite keen. I might have one or two of these leaflets in my loft gathering more dust.

I suppose that, during that war, the RAF intelligence worked in Bush House before the BBC became resident. At least the last RAF person to leave did put the light out. I'm off to wash my hands again now just at the thought of those cobwebs.

David Carlsen

Emergency Control Room

When I was 12 years old the fear of an atomic war seemed very real. We knew we'd have four minutes to prepare, and what better way to spend them – and the last four minutes of a rather boring lesson – than by drawing a map of Europe on a scrap of paper and plotting the course of an imaginary intercontinental ballistic missile from Moscow to Aberdeen Grammar School. The school, being built of granite, might have survived rather better than some parts of Bush. Notably, the Emergency Control Room.

As a junior studio manager, one had to carry out a variety of unlikely and sometimes unwanted tasks, including being delegated by the duty operations manager to search through studios for bombs. This was not as worrying as it sounds. It seemed unlikely that a bomber would have got past the watchful eyes of the commissionaires at the Centre Block reception. Many of them were ex-Navy officers: charming, courteous men. But you wouldn't want to mess with them. As far as I know, the only damage that ever occurred was done to a studio by a group of over-enthusiastic Welsh nationalists.

One morning, signing in for my shift, I saw that the schedulers had put two of us down to check the Emergency Control Room – down to a basement, out through a door, and along a dusty corridor littered with what might have been rat droppings. (They probably were: the water table at Bush was high, being near the Thames, and rats were attracted by scraps in the basement canteen or the club.) The main control room was on the sixth floor, and thus subject to the blast wave of a 10-megaton thermonuclear attack. The Emergency Control Room, on the other hand, would apparently be safe, because it was down a flight of steps behind a nice solid wood door. So, I supposed, ran the logic of someone, somewhere, but I was not entirely convinced. Once down in it, rows of lights glowed reassuringly, waiting for the day when, after the control room was hit, any remaining studio managers or technical assistants would stream through that wooden door, down the stairs and resume transmissions – though not as normal.

Hamish Norbrook

Glimpses of Other Worlds

For a naïve 22-year-old English girl, arriving at Bush House in the summer of 1968 was a seismic experience. London in the swinging sixties was exciting enough but, once through the portals of Bush House, life would never be the same again. Coming through the doors of Centre Block, into the lofty spaces of the entrance hall and stairwell, the noise of London would gradually recede till you were transported into another dimension. No need to go travelling round the world, the world was here in all its variety of culture, languages, history, ideas and intensity.

1968 was the year of the Prague Spring, when, for a brief moment, it seemed as if eastern Europe was opening up. But when Russian tanks rolled into Czechoslovakia that summer, the fallout was felt right round the world. And it was a sharp and salient introduction to a world so far removed from the cosy postwar life of suburban north London. As they carried on broadcasting their way through terrible news, well aware of what was happening in their country and to their families and friends, the faces of my Czech and Slovak colleagues brought home to me the fragility of a taken-for-granted normality which existed in the UK.

As weeks, months and years went on, and I got to know Bush House people, my respect could only increase. Many were refugees and exiles, often having experienced unimaginable events in their homelands, never able to return there. Others fell into the category of mildly eccentric veering towards completely mad. But what united them was an unshakable commitment to the ideal of freedom of thought and expression and the desire to communicate with consummate professionalism even in the most challenging of circumstances.

And if it all sounds deadly serious, on one level it was; at the same time, Bush House was a joyous and happy place, where humour was frequently used to diffuse tension and stress and where real characters abounded and were accepted in this close-knit egalitarian community.

The canteen at lunchtime was a hub of noisy activity, where engineers, secretaries, studio managers, broadcasters and senior managers, even the managing director, queued together for international food before sitting down to exchange gossip and intrigue, which then flew around the canteen, into the club and up and down the lifts within minutes. Several times an hour, a telephonist would announce over the tannoy, "Akram Saleh to box 2, please" and an urbane gentleman would rise from his seat and saunter over to a booth, set against the back wall of the canteen, to take a phone call. Why was Akram Saleh called to the phone so often and by whom? The questions were never answered.

At night, Bush House became a quieter place but the transmission caravan rolled on. Offices and corridors were deserted but, in the studios, weary broadcasters and studio managers found ways to keep themselves awake during long tapes. An Iranian girl talked of her experiences of exile in London; two Latin Americans laughed so much that they could not sit in the studio together and had to take turns to read the news; a Frenchman described with longing the beauty of his home town of Beirut and Lebanon; another Frenchman extolled the pleasures of camping in a tiny tent in the south of France; an Indonesian transmission opened with a recording of birdsong; a Nepali broadcaster started his programme by singing; a Bulgarian talked of his passion for freedom and his desire to make his voice heard.

At the end of the night, the trudge home over Waterloo Bridge, with the sun coming up over the city, the mind mulling over the night just ending. Tiny glimpses of other worlds, other places, different lives lodged in the imagination, never to be forgotten. The perspective shifted: narrow, parochial views dissolved into nothingness; and, for one young English girl, life would never be the same again. And thank God for that.

Jane Wood

Mother Is Listening

The BBC Hausa Service was and still is part of Nigerian culture – I grew up listening to it with my parents. I became more and more interested in working for the BBC because of what I used to hear, because I admired the presenters. Most of them, back in Africa, tend to be very big stars, in some cases bigger than Beckham here. So I just sent in my CV. Someone gave me the address. I had done some journalism before for about a year. Eventually, they got back to me to say they were interested in my application but there wasn't a vacancy. So I kept doing my stuff at my radio station, and then they invited me to tests and interviews, and I went along.

Imagine how happy my mum was when I got a job here. Listening to the BBC was a pleasure for her, but when her own son started presenting it absolutely amazed my mum. When I got promoted to a management role she really doubted whether I still worked at the BBC. I had to call her and say, "Hi mum, I'm still here." She scolded me, "Why aren't you on air?" And nowadays whenever I go back on holiday she still tells me exactly what I should say and how I should say it and corrects my every error.

Isa Abba Adamu

Keeping an Eye on All the Indians

One morning when I came to the office, my secretary told me, "There was a call for you from Scotland Yard and the caller would like you to ring him back." I became nervous and wondered what could be wrong. I tried to remember my movements on previous days, then I rang the chap to arrange a meeting, and he came to see me. The inspector wanted to know about the telegram sent to Hyderabad which said: "Broadcasting next week, please listen on 12, 18, 21 and 23." This, he said, sounded like a code. I explained that it was quite simple: when students record a message, you can't give them the exact date of a broadcast, so we give them a number of possible dates when their message would be included in the programme. Apparently, this student wanted his family to listen to his message on all those days. This satisfied the inspector. He then sat there chatting, enquiring about my various colleagues who were not there at the time. I was rather surprised and asked him how on earth he knew them. He said that it was his job to keep an eye on all the Indians in London, who they were, what they did and where they got their money from.

Iqbal Bahadur Sarin

Down With Britain!

The first time I came to the BBC I was invited to take part in a women's programme. They were discussing divorce and one of the ladies there – there were no ladies among the staff at that moment, she was from outside – said, "We don't like divorce in India. Down with Britain! India is number one!" I was so stunned I started looking around, petrified somebody would come and drag them outside, but nobody said anything. Later on, I said to the editor, "Of course you're going to edit it?" "Why, that's her opinion," he replied. "If she says 'Down with Britain', she says 'Down with Britain'. There's nothing political. It's divorce! Why should I take it out?"

Rajni Kaul

Whoooosh!

We had a magnificent technical facility called Lamson tubes. You would roll this piece of paper, somebody would stamp it – for instance, I'm sending it to the Hungarian Service, so my clerk would go and stamp "Hungarian" on it, then I would ring him up saying, I'm sending you the new story on, let's say, floods in China. And there was a tremendous "whooooosh": you put it in the tube and it went to the far ends of the building.

Mary Raine

Dangers of the Lamson Tube

In the distant days before computers, when paper really was the only material of communication, news bulletins were taken by subeditors to language translators. Updates would be delivered in the same way, by hand. That worked fine for many years until it was decided to move several language sections, including the South European Service, to the North East wing of Bush House. As news subeditors were busy people, it was deemed inappropriate to expect them to descend several floors, walk across the courtyard and either go up several more floors or wait for reluctant lifts to arrive, to hand over a news bulletin and repeat the process for any updates (of which there could often be several per bulletin). So a device called the Lamson tube was installed. I'm not sure how the tube worked exactly but it was something to do with compressed air in a confined space which propelled a canister from the newsroom to its destination. The subeditors would compile the bulletin, roll it up in a canister and send it on its way to the North East wing. And when the translator had finished, he or she would sign the front page to show that they had indeed translated the bulletin and then return it to the newsroom via the Lamson tube.

Those language sections which had both a late night and a dawn transmission often used the same news translator for both, with the unlucky individual spending the night in one of Bush House's dormitories. Having dragged himself (usually it was a man) from his bed and collected a press review from the array of trays stationed on each landing, which were delivered by hand by the Distribution Unit (mostly ladies), and duly translated it, our Greek (or it may have been Turkish) colleague went to collect a bulletin from the Lamson tube. Not having yet fully woken up, it was not until he was halfway through his translation that it began to dawn on him that the news stories were alarmingly familiar. He rang the newsroom to enquire why he had been sent the same stories as the night before. "You haven't," insisted the newsroom. "You've got a completely new bulletin. We'll send you another copy." In spite of the shortage of time, our colleague was able to translate the correct bulletin in time. On his return from the studio, he checked the front page of the first bulletin he had been sent. There was his signature – it was the previous night's bulletin.

Yes, you've guessed it! The previous night's bulletin had never arrived back in the newsroom and when the next morning's edition was sent, it just propelled the old one back along the tube. All news translators were very careful to inspect the front pages of their bulletins from then on.

Angela Carte

A Poke With a Broom Handle

As a transmission deadline approached, the Sports Department (second floor, South East wing) complained that the newsroom (fourth floor, South East wing) weren't sending them any sports stories down the chute. Yes, the pipe joining the two offices was blocked with dozens of news agency reports. A poke with a broom handle, a brief panic in the sports room – but the listener wouldn't have noticed the difference.

Hugh Saxby

"This Is How My Mother Must Have Talked to Me"

I remember at the start of the Christmas holidays in 1971, something happened that made me feel very good. It was on Sunday, my children's programme recording day, when somebody said there was a big package for me. We used to get listener's letters and as I was only coming in three days a week then, it was kept in a corner. I opened it and found a postcard which I can describe as one of the best fan letters in all 40 years of my broadcasting career. This letter came from Hardwar, a Hindu holy city, where many people who renounce normal life and are called sadhus, ascetics, beggars. Maybe the city is popular with sadhus because millions of Hindu pilgrims visit Hardwar every year and give alms to these people who spend most of their time praying. Anyway, this letter was from one of the sadhus, because he wrote his name underneath: Swami Devananda. It started, "Rajni-didi," – "didi" means sister – "I have never known my mother. I don't know what she called me, but listening to your children's programme last Sunday when you addressed the listeners, 'My beloved children, lots of love,' I felt this is how my mother must have talked to me. Your voice was so full of motherly love that I couldn't help weeping." Then the listener further explained that he, along with some other sadhus of the area where the Bangladesh war was being fought, had started gathering around every evening near a small shop in the city which had a radio, and they all listened to the BBC to get the real news about the war, and that was how he came across my children's programme. He said, "We have renounced the world, but we still want to hear about our ex-homeland." So that is how effective the BBC was. These people had given up their normal homes, but once the war started, they had to hear about it. He used these very words, "real news about our homeland."

Rajni Kaul

Remnants of the Raj

When I came back to the Urdu service in 1970, after a hectic spell of film-making between 1966 and 1970, I came to a different world. From 200 Oxford via Alexandra Palace, I arrived at the portals of Bush House. If in Oxford Street and Alexandra Palace we had the luxury of riding in a lift operated by attendants, Bush House by then had entered the technological age. There were self-operating lifts with their own built-in sound effects that did not announce the floors, nor did they relay the latest news, thank God.

I noticed that the Raj mindset had begun to fade, and we had a lively atmosphere in the Eastern Service, as it was then called, with one important proviso: news and comment were strictly controlled by the remnants of the Raj. Outside of that, namely in the Arts and Culture Department, we had all the freedom to manoeuvre. But current affairs were firmly under the thumb of the white brigade. The language services, at least as far as I know – Hindi, Bengali, Urdu, Burmese, Sinhalese, Tamil, Nepali, etc. – had no reporters of our own in the field. We received no despatches in Urdu, we were bound to use only the despatches of English-speaking correspondents and reporters, which we translated into Urdu. We were delivered, from the rarefied heights of the newsroom, individual items of news for our respective bulletins. We were even sent the news order, all this by hand from the newsroom via a messenger service that occasionally created hilarious situations, as we approached the deadline to rush to some distant studio on a different floor or in a different building.

Yavar Abbas

Busy Production

One of the most difficult jobs on a drama production is that of the chief studio manager. When I worked in radio drama there were usually three studio managers on a production: one drove the sound-mixing desk, one played in sound effects – from tape or vinyl in my day – and one would make the necessary "noises off": for example, clinking glasses, opening doors, stabbing cabbages (to make the realistic sound of a person being killed without having to decimate the ranks of Equity too much).

On a production of Noel Coward's *Brief Encounter* (using the film script rather than the play, and starring Ian Holm and Cheryl Campbell) we had Nicky Barranger, who had worked on a number of drama productions and was very talented, but this was her first time as the senior studio manager on the desk.

Those of you who know the story can imagine that it was a very busy production aurally. There's the station café where the two lovers meet, so plenty of clinking crockery, lots of walking up and down the platforms – at one point I was roped in to make the appropriate walking sounds as I had hard-soled shoes on – and, of course, the various steam trains entering and leaving the station – not to mention the all-important words from the actors.

Trying to balance all these sounds coming from a variety of inputs would have challenged even the most experienced, but we thought Nicky was managing very well until it got to day two when she confided in us: "I couldn't work out what I was doing wrong: I kept trying to fade down the train and it just wouldn't fade – until I woke up and realised that the train in question was going past the bottom of my garden."

Rosemary Grave

Sonnets at Night

There were some brilliant people working for the Monitoring Service. The one to become most famous after the war was Ernst Gombrich, the distinguished art historian. Gombrich and I got on very well and sometimes, when we were both on night shift and nothing much was happening, we competed with each other translating Petrarch's sonnets.

Ewald Osers

An Epidemic of Writing

I wrote my first book recently – all thanks to Bush House. I carried the book with me from my home in Kashmir to Delhi and then on to London. It only became possible for me to finish it because the two people who recruited me in Delhi, Sam Miller and Mohammed Hanif, went on to publish their books, and both of them are famous authors now. If fact, there is an epidemic in the Urdu Service – actually, we have too many people writing. We may have to ask them to concentrate on their day jobs a little more!

Waheed Mirza

Shift Work

I always had the need and the desire to write, and my other activities enabled this. Imagine all these lives, all these personae, all these jobs, some paid, some unpaid – without a private income you have to top up what you are earning. I spent 23 years at Bush House. It clearly had something going for it because of all the jobs I've ever had, it gave me the most possibilities to lead my other lives. Why? The key word is shift work. My life would not have been possible without it. One small book I published was by Keith Bosley, who wrote some of his most important works on night shift when no one was looking – but then nobody was looking, except me, occasionally. Bosley wrote the book, I published it and it was printed by a newsroom editor called Derek Maggs, who had a printing press at home, so the entire book was a Bush House creation, and we could correct proofs in the middle of the night.

Anthony Rudolf

Bush Couples

Bush House was not just a place for international broadcasting. Staff, particularly language service staff, wrote and translated books and poetry there. There is a reasonably well substantiated anecdote from the 1950s that a member of the Hungarian Service challenged a colleague to a duel, having argued vigorously over a translation. That really is taking work seriously.

Incidentally, several wives and husbands met each other there. One or two language service staff members had something of a reputation, which was not helped by the fact that extensive night working meant that there were beds located all over the building. Only the soundest of sleepers and snorers slept in the official dormitory in the North East wing.

Hugh Saxby

Love Among the Razor Blades

The byways of broadcasting journalism are littered with remembered kisses and useless ephemera. *Love Among the Razor Blades* (LATRB) contained many of the former and represents an excellent example of the latter. It took the form of a serial romantic novel, largely based at Bush House ("the glamorous international nerve-centre of the fabled BBC World Service") and appeared periodically for around 25 years. The now obscure title dates back to the days of editing tape on a block with a razor blade.

The authors – and in its origins at Broadcasting House there were several, among them a future cabinet minister – adhered rigorously to a few guiding principles. Crucially, every chapter had to be positively stuffed with the time-honoured clichés of the romantic serial genre – and in this the authors succeeded triumphantly. "Unbridled passion" was a favourite, though sadly it was often tricky to weave in the likes of "hail of bullets" or "wall of silence". (Critics of these LATRB shortcomings were, however, able to take great comfort from the contemporary newsroom output, unencumbered by the editorial constraints that bedevil the authors of romantic fiction.)

Each chapter of LATRB stated clearly that it was "A Work of Fiction". The pages were indeed peopled by non-existent glitterati of international public service broadcasting. Nevertheless, confusion was apt to arise because the characters in LATRB – Mary Hockaday, for example, or Andrew Whitehead – often bore the same names as important real-life BBC figures. The more naïve and credulous readers would sometimes ask, "But did Mary Hockaday *really* do that?" Clarification on these basic points was hard to come by. The authors cloaked themselves with the nom de plume Violet Conn – an even more obscure echo of the Bush House past: the Green and Violet Cons were respectively the main and back-up news continuity studios. Happily or not, the vast bulk of the entire LATRB manuscript still exists.

Oliver Scott

Common Facilities

When I started at the BBC in August 1974 I joined what was then called the Russian Section of the External Services. Our immediate neighbours were the Bulgarian, Yugoslav and Romanian Sections. There were also central talks writers – a rather élite group that wrote material centrally for the whole of Bush House. And there was Anatol Goldberg, the External Services' chief commentator, who wrote analytical talks in English but broadcast almost every day in Russian and, very often, in German and French as well. The Reference Library occupied a large chunk of the territory in the heart of the Russian Section, so there was a constant coming and going of programme assistants from every section in Bush House.

Apart from the loos with their dark, heavy, varnished wooden doors, there were some important common facilities. There was one self-op studio shared by all the sections on a rota basis. Next to it was a room which contained the Banda machine, a hand-cranked device which duplicated pale purple copies of scripts by means of wax stencils and alcoholic spirit. It was an extreme fire hazard at a time when smoking everywhere was the norm. Curiously, small fires broke out quite frequently in self-op studios when cigarette ends fell into bins full of recording tape but never, in my recollection, in the Banda room. The age of the photocopier had not yet dawned.

The other vitally important common area was the large landing in front of the lifts. On display tables by the railings a line of in-trays was arranged. There was a tray for central newsroom stories and another for correspondent dispatches. There were also separate trays for yellow tops, red tops and purple tops. The colour ran across the top of the document and gave a broad indication of its genre. Yellow tops were topical talks on subjects which included arts and human interest. Purple tops were full-blown features, usually aimed at weekend programmes, so a new one came out every Thursday. Science was red. Economics in 1974 had little status – and therefore no colour – despite the massive oil price hikes the previous year.

Feeding these in-trays, day and night, was a group of messengers who distributed paper in the right quantities in the right in-trays. The principal consumers were programme organisers and editors who would come out periodically to check what was on offer and then return to their offices with a sheaf of papers. If it was still early in the day they might take them down to the canteen for perusal over coffee, decide which to include in their transmissions and sub them minimally before handing them to a programme assistant to be translated.

News bulletins were too important to be distributed through the in-trays on the landing and a duty news translator had to go to the newsroom in person to collect and sign for them. The newsroom brooked no deviation or alteration – except occasionally by negotiation. To use today's jargon, content was almost entirely paper-based and hardly anyone used telephones to gather programme material. New recruits were trained in the art of interviewing and using a Uher portable tape recorder, but in the language sections interviews were still exceptional and were regarded with some suspicion.

The marble on the landing was a kind of off-cream colour, scored and pitted, and on it gathered the dirt from the polluted air (traffic outside, smokers inside and no air conditioning except in studios and the control room), mixed in turn with the wax and spirit of the Banda machine. Corridors were lined with wooden partitions glazed above waist level with thick frosted glass. Doors made a crashing noise as you opened and closed them. Open windows let out the smoke, but let in noise and dirt. The tannoy system constantly broadcast news snaps and told us which ring main point to use to listen to a correspondent filing a dispatch. Translators were dictating to language typists in almost every room. And mechanical typewriters generated their own clatter. Even on the courtyard side of the building the noise was invasive.

If you came out of the lifts, turned left and left again, you came to the Russian Section, and this three-sides-of-a-square route was the way everyone was meant to go. However, if you turned right as you came out of the lifts, there was another pair of doors, followed by a small anteroom with a single desk and a typewriter. This was where the Russian news typist sat and took dictation from the news translator. The anteroom was also a shortcut to the Russian Section, so the news translator was constantly being disturbed. I have a powerful memory of a particular news translator, a non-smoker, who chewed raw garlic when he felt a cold or a sore throat coming on. The smell was overwhelming and the news typists were in the front line. No one took the shortcut on garlic days.

David Morton

Saucy Stories

The Bush dormitories were in the basement of the North East wing and provided sleeping accommodation to those working overnight. When I started at Bush in

1995 saucy stories abounded about men slinking into the women's dormitory and vice versa. I witnessed no such encounters – though on my second visit to the dormitory I saw what was either a large mouse or a small rat scrambling across the entrance. I told the security guard on duty but he didn't seem particularly surprised.

The security guards would come in and wake you at an hour you gave them. This was done with the use of a torch which would be shone directly in your eyes and, if that failed, with a verbal alert. The rest of the dormitory remained in darkness so there were always shadowy figures coming in or going out.

The beds in the men's dormitory were separated by thin partitions and curtains. Bed linen was BBC regulation: starchy and always with some holes. The floral bedspreads were covered in stains. The thin screens between beds did nothing to dampen the noise – in fact, they somehow magnified it. Grunting, groaning, snoring – and worse – seemed pretty constant. It reminded me of my boarding school sanatorium.

The dormitories shut down two or three years after I started working at Bush, presumably to make way for shifts that did not allow for such long breaks between duties.

David Austin

"Hello, Darling! Sorry, I'm Held up at Waterloo!"

I was editing late one day in a studio when a somewhat dishevelled colleague rushed in, his shirt flapping out of his trousers, a tell-tale smear of lipstick plainly visible on his shirt collar. "You keep discs of sound effects here, don't you? Could you just play me EC 48B? It's the one of Waterloo Station at the rush hour." A trifle bemused, I did as he requested, and as the studio cubicle resounded to the sound of train announcements and on-rushing commuters, he whipped out his mobile phone. "Hello darling! Sorry, I'm held up at Waterloo. There's been some incident at Clapham Junction and trains are all running late. I'll be home as soon as I can." He finished the call and gave me a guilty smirk. "Sorry about that, Gordon. Needs must..."

Gordon House

Arkle Is Dead

I came down to the canteen one morning to find Ahkram Saleh (arguably the most popular man from the Arabic Section at the time) with his head on his arms on the table, tears pouring down his face. I quickly offered any help I could. "He's dead," said Ahkram. Naturally, I thought he was speaking of a member of his family. "Who is dead?" I asked gently, holding his hand. "Arkle," he said and proceeded to give me a five-minute paean to one of the most famous horses ever to win races for this betting man. He explained that it was because of the shame the horse felt at having been gelded, which made Arkle run so fast – to prove his masculinity despite his disgrace.

Lynne Plummer

Censor Button, Temptingly Close

When I recall Bush House, my mental image is that of a giant ocean liner cruising through the dark, lights blazing into night as its crew labours to keep the engines turning and its officers attempt to steer a steady course. I entered this ship, this fortress – to be interviewed by a tall skinny man with a gammy leg and an enigmatic name. I don't remember his exact title but he was, in effect, second in command of the Russian and East European division of the World Service, the only one that employed language supervisors.

In truth I had come to the interview with a great deal of scepticism and became even more doubtful when I heard that supervisors had a political role – to ensure that broadcasts to countries behind the Iron Curtain went out as written by the BBC news editors. But my interviewer insisted that my role in the process would be purely technical and produced some stunning facts about the flexible nature of the job.

A few weeks later I returned to the ship and reported to the officer in charge of the unit, Walter Morison, on one of the upper floors of Bush House. Between us we were expected to cover broadcasts in Russian, Polish, Czech, Slovak, Hungarian, Romanian, Bulgarian, Serbo-Croatian and Slovene. Our job was to read the translations of the main news bulletin and the political commentary that was broadcast daily by each section, check that they stayed faithful to the original and make sure the translators didn't smuggle any hidden messages into them.

Soon after that I accompanied my first band of broadcasters to one of the studios located in the basement of Bush House, where it truly felt as if we were in the bowels of an ocean liner, and sat beside them to ensure that they followed the translations I had just checked upstairs. In the folklore of the World Service, this system was introduced after an émigré broadcaster had run amok in the studio and started shouting political insults and obscenities into the microphone. The story was gospel in Bush House, and the upshot was that each studio was equipped with a so-called censor button, which, when pressed, instantly cut off all sound from the microphones. The only person endowed with the authority to press it in mid-broadcast was the language supervisor, i.e. me.

In fact, I never used the button then, nor on any subsequent occasion, nor heard of anyone using it for this weighty purpose. I idly wondered what would happen if I did cut someone off (that button was a temptingly short distance from my index finger), but for better or worse that never happened.

Michael Scammell

Tribute Where Tribute Is Due

I must pay some tribute to our supervisors, who included quite a few well-known writers. It seems that literary people unsuitable, for some reason or other, for active military service, were directed by the authorities into the BBC or the Ministry of Information. Some of these supervisors, after butchering our generally poor English, would seek us out afterwards and with great kindness explain where we offended against grammar or syntax or style.

Ewald Osers

Public Enemy Number One

The Russian Service had a dedicated language supervisor, who was public enemy number one. One day several of his colleagues got together and presented him with a piece of paper. It was a master copy or rather, a master sheet produced by the duplicating system we had then, which just looked like a typed script. Anyway, there was this sheet labelled "Insert for literary magazine" and he processed it in the usual way, leaving no sentence unturned. When his colleagues saw it they said, "Didn't you know that it's Chekhov?" To which he replied, "Anton Pavlovich made mistakes too, you know."

Milada Haigh

Recruitment Staff in Marigolds

Way back in the early 1990s, before the introduction of online job applications and even emails, the BBC World Service Recruitment were doing what they do best, a large producer campaign for one of the language services. This one was for the Swahili Service and an advert had been placed in the local press asking for CVs to be sent to London. The response was excellent, with over 400 CVs received – on what were often the best scraps of paper applicants could muster. Each was carefully logged, by hand, on a paper spreadsheet, and kept in a cardboard box. However, one morning, the recruitment advisor dealing with it (and no, it wasn't me!) came in to find the box had gone. It was nowhere to be found, but then realisation dawned: the bins had been emptied that morning; the box was under a desk, next to the bin – surely not?

Desperate calls to the facilities management ensued. "Oh yes, anything left on the floor would have been taken away as rubbish!" came the reply, "by now it will be in the compactor in the car park. We don't have access to it – we will have to get Westminster council to come and open it for you." A few hours later that's exactly what happened and the contents of the compactor was strewn over the car park; pink marigold gloves were handed out to the members of the Recruitment team and a desperate search began. About two thirds of the CVs were recovered and laid to dry around the office. It was quite a sight to see the Recruitment staff in their marigolds picking through the rubbish heap, resembling a BBC documentary on street kids ("they live off the refuse of others"). We even made it into *Private Eye* – a paragraph on BBC employees seen rummaging through bins – under a headline of "BBC scraping the bottom of the barrel" or words to that effect.

The campaign was extended to allow the lost CVs to be re-sent. But the nicest part of the story was when Huseyin Sukan, the then head of the Turkish Service, came into our office later that afternoon with a box of cakes from Patisserie Valerie and said, "Now you can either remember this as the day you rummaged through the bins or the day you ate nice cakes."

Suzanne Luu

"For Heaven's Sake, Woman!"

Back in the days when mobile phones were the size and weight of a house brick and very rare, the newsroom bought one to test and gave it to the then World Service political correspondent, Geoff Robertson (formerly Lally). The mischievous Geoff handed the Correspondents Unit secretary, Gail Styles, a slip of paper and instructed her to "Ring me on that number at 1:15pm, please." He then crossed the road to the Waldorf Hotel, placed the mobile prominently on the bar and ordered a pint and a sandwich. "Brnng, brnng," went the mobile at exactly 1:15pm. Geoff picked it up, listened to it briefly, then announced loudly (loud was Geoff's default voice level), "For heaven's sake, woman! How many times do I have to tell you not to phone me at the office!"

Ian Richardson

Breakfast Egg in Kipper Water

The Bush House canteen could be counted as a hazard. One cook had the habit of estimating how much toast she would require for the night and doing that number on one side. When you ordered she toasted the other side, with predictable results. One morning she boiled the announcer Peter King's breakfast egg in kipper water. He threw it at her – it hit the pillar behind the cash register.

Roger Wilmut

Neither Eager nor Flurried

The self-op news studio used to open off the back of the newsroom, but the newsreaders were kept in another part of Bush. They would generally wander up at about five minutes to air – it was a matter of professional pride to look neither eager nor flurried – but every now and again they mistimed it.

On one of these rare occasions, with two minutes to go, there was no newsreader. Frantic calls were made. Nothing! And then, with less than a minute to spare our man burst in, panting and bright red in the face. The lift had broken down, and he had run up many stairs. He was a genial, bohemian man of a fuller figure and this was a heroic effort; the whole room was mesmerised as he raced for the back of the room, only to find the studio locked. In despair, he hammered fruitlessly on the door until someone recovered their wits enough to break it to him that he was trying to get into the stationery cupboard – the studio was the next door along.

Jessica Macfarlane

Temps Perdu à la Recherche

A new and officious colleague, whose high opinion of herself did not match her abilities and who would not last long at the French Section, entered the lift as we were descending to the canteen and announced breathlessly: "I am going to the library to do some research for I am being sent to the Proust exhibition tomorrow to file a report." As she left the lift, one of us observed, "Temps perdu à la recherche."

Ninon Leader

When the Entire World Seemed to Stop Still

Day and night were different. The day shift ran according to rules and procedures controlled, more or less benignly, by managers. But the night shift remained something of a mystery to me as a newly appointed manager. It was, apparently, off bounds.

During the daytime you could feel relatively important, check a script, question a news story, carry a clipboard, that sort of thing. But the night was mysterious, it operated according to its own secret codes. Managers were kept at a distance. There were two large transmissions, starting at midnight and then again at 3am. They just happened, with no managers or editors to fuss around and get in the way. The hardened veterans of the night shift kept their operations secret. Many pre-recorded programmes were played out on quarter-inch tape from the transmission studios, and the news had to be done live. Sometimes a big news story would force the updating or replacement of a pre-recorded programme. If so, very laconic notes were left in the overnight log, explaining what had happened. Somehow they always gave the sense that the full story had not been told.

Every now and then information would slip out. A former producer won one of Mexico's top literary prizes. The gossip was that most of that novel had actually been written on the Bush House night shift. I didn't know whether to feel proud of that literary achievement, by a sort of indirect association, or worried that the allegations would bring new scrutiny from the time-and-motion brigade. The night shifters got not inconsiderable payments for working antisocial hours and also received something called LNEM – late night/early morning transport allowance. That meant a taxi home at 5am. The night-timers protected these benefits fiercely.

The staff at Bush broke down into various tribes and categories. Apart from nationalities and cliques, there were those who never worked nights, those who did both days and nights, a versatile bunch, and a hard core of "night shift-onlies". Some of these were staffers, some long-standing freelancers or casuals. Some fortified themselves for their ordeal with hard liquor from the BBC Club down in the basement. One member of the night shift-only hard core was a veteran distinguished Colombian broadcaster of deep, authoritative voice and indeterminate age. The age thing bothered me, as some rulebook somewhere said we shouldn't employ anyone over the age of 60. He was well past that, but with charm and determination resisted all attempts to establish his real age. He had been on the staff at some point, but his personnel records were suspiciously missing. Every now and then some visiting Latin American dignitary would make worrisome references to how his unmistakeable voice was heard on short wave during the Second World War. I occasionally tried to work out a timeline, but recoiled in doubt when it suggested he had to be in his seventies, or maybe his eighties.

So things went on until someone broke the code of night-shift silence to tell me there was a problem with our much beloved Colombian newsreader. They were embarrassed to bring such a matter to management but the problem was – and they hoped and sought assurances that they wouldn't be quoted on this – that he was falling asleep during live transmissions. At the time we were doing double-headed news presentation. One presenter read one story, the other presenter the next. Both newsreaders sat across a desk, with a big old-fashioned BBC microphone hanging down from the roof between them, and green and red lights on the table to tell you when you were on air.

My source explained. The man will read the lead story in a clear, strong, sonorous voice: "In the Soviet Union, the leader of the Communist Party Mikhail Gorbachev has stated that…" – but unfortunately at exactly that point his head slumps down, the hand holding the script goes limp and he closes his eyes. There is a dead silence, punctured only by his heavy relaxed breathing, as if he is in a yoga trance. One second goes by, two, three. I look through the studio window at the studio manager at the controls, and we exchange looks of desperation. I think: do I read the rest of the sentence? Do we go to tape? Do I cut in and apologise for technical difficulties? And just as the situation becomes unbearable, his head snaps back up absolutely straight, his eyes open with a new shine, and he bursts out in staccato form: "…the period of openness or perestroika is only just beginning and there will be further reforms put before the State Council." And so the news bulletin went on in this stop-start way, with mid-sentence pauses when the entire world seemed to stop still, at least within the confines of studio C26. Perhaps it gave us a distinctive sound.

Andrew Thompson

Nighty Night

When I was a studio manager at Bush House in the 1980s, we used to cheer up our long nightshifts by sometimes agreeing to come to work in fancy dress. When the theme was "Vicars and Tarts", a World Service announcer came as a cardinal and chased a friend of mine, dressed as a vicar, all round a studio. One night the dress code was "Pyjamas". And in a flimsy nighty I went to work on 24 Hours (the predecessor to Newshour). Sometimes when you were doing this shift there was a chance to sleep for a few hours in a dormitory. I was working with a colleague who had a teddy bear and a toothbrush in his top dressing gown pocket. When we got to the studio the current affairs producer looked worried and said, "You can't go to bed yet, we've got work to do."

Kate Howells

"My Friends, It's All an Illusion"

Strike action at the BBC is rare, but when all journalists are called out, this puts many language staff in a very difficult situation. They know that their listeners, living in countries where fair information is not everyday fare, make regular dates with the half-hours of the Burmese Service or the Pashtos, the Somalis or the Hausas. So for those broadcasters coming to Bush House to meet their huge audiences across the airwaves, a strike felt like an abnegation of a public duty to which they were deeply dedicated.

One particular strike was a heated one, called because an arm of the BBC had been using untrained staff paid at low rates. People really did feel angered at this. Some of us went down to ensure that our colleagues could get through the picket line if they so wished. The Burmese Service hurried in, eyes down – gentle broadcasters – as they were harangued. The Pashtos walked quickly in, heads held high; the Vietnamese split and argued; others dithered or turned away.

Then down from a double-decker bus stepped the slight but dapper figure or Mr Shankamurthi, senior producer of the Tamil Service. As he approached, a very large picket stood in front of him and said: "Blackleg labour, brother, and we are asking for six percent!"

Shanka hoisted his umbrella up on one arm and put his palms together in a high namaste. "Six percent, sixteen percent, sixty percent – my friends, it's all an illusion, you see, a mere distraction in the court of higher values."

The pickets fell back. Shanka swept in. But he was, we knew, not thinking of peace negotiations for his beleaguered audience in northern Sri Lanka. Nor was he thinking of the world ecological crisis followed by his loyal listeners in Tamil Nadu. No! Shanka had more pressing work to hand. He had not yet completed his task of translating all of *Macbeth* into Tamil. He had already given his audience, in a large number of instalments, his *Hamlet* and his *Lear*, and indeed his *Pygmalion*. He knew how eagerly his version of the Scottish play was anticipated. He walked swiftly up to the seventh floor of Centre Block, carrying his lunch in a bag.

Barry Langridge

A Bit of a Lark

One of the World Service drama productions was a recording of Vaclav Havel's *The Memorandum* directed by Gordon House in 1980, with Michael Gambon and Ian Richardson in the cast. In this play the deputy manager of a large organisation has introduced an artificial language of gobbledegook into the office: Ptydepe (pronounced "puh-TYE-duh-pee", I believe).

After a somewhat fraught recording session, with most of the actors struggling at some point with the pronunciation of this word, the cast and crew (always ready for a drink at the best of times) had repaired to the Bush House Club for a relaxing evening.

In those days there used to be a commissionaire on the door to sign in non-members and to take phone calls – this was, of course, before the advent of mobile phones. This gentleman often mispronounced our unfamiliar names when he opened the mic to page someone.

So a few of the actors thought it would be a bit of a lark if they rang up and asked this man to page Mr Ptydepe, while the assembled drama company waited, expecting to have a good laugh at the poor chap's expense. Apparently, though, the joke backfired, as the said commissionaire pronounced the name perfectly in just one take! We only employ professionals here at Bush, you know. But I can't help wondering if our budding actor ever found out about the trick that had been played on him.

Rosemary Grave

Learning on the Job

You felt pretty small when you passed for the first time between the imposing ionic columns of Bush House. You felt even smaller when you realised how little you knew about making radio programmes. You joined the World Service with a certain expertise – in my case teaching English as a foreign language – but within days you were made aware that the connection between what you knew and what you had to know in order to make a programme that was fit for transmission seemed unbridgeable.

You had to learn how to use a razor blade (we were all given a box of blades in week one). A radio programme had to be 14:30 minutes long and in order to get it to that length you had to cut it, literally, with a blade to fit the desired length and then close the gap with some sticky tape. And the bit you cut out? It joined the seaweed-like pile of tape on the floor ready to be disposed of until... oops! that gem in your interview was somewhere in that messy pile.

You had to learn to be thorough. I well remember listening to my own programme as it was broadcast in the presence of the then programme organiser who pointed out that I'd left in an "unedited re-take". In other words, when an actor or a presenter fluffed (another technical term) in the studio, it was your job to edit out the mistake, that is, mark the spot on the tape with a yellow crayon and then cut it out. It was easy to let that thing slide when you were hot and tired in the tiny editing cubicle and the programme had to be ready for broadcast in an hour.

You had to learn to stay within budget. You were often sent on courses but almost always when it was too late and you'd spent months of uncertainty making blind attempts to find out who all these people you were paying for were and how someone could spend so much on a duty tour. A duty tour? An astonishing offer by your superior for you to travel somewhere with a view to learning something. Not to be confused with grace leave, an even more generous opportunity for you to go somewhere without even the pretence of learning anything. Ah, those were the days when you could ask your secretary to book lunch for you and your studio guest at one of those pleasant restaurants around Covent Garden. If you couldn't get into PJ's or Joe Allen's, it was usually because the Russian or the Brazilian Section had booked a table before you.

You had to learn what your wavelengths were. Each section in Bush House had certain transmission times and wavelengths. Most sections had two or three allocated slots per day or night. As an English teaching department, we provided a bilingual programme to fit into the output of most of the 40 or so language sections – amazing how quickly you learned to detect an unedited re-take in Urdu, Farsi and Russian – but we also transmitted many hours of English programmes that went out with their own wavelengths and time slots. These precious times were constantly being poached by other ambitious section heads. Mastering the wall-sized charts of different transmissions was virtually impossible. The half-dozen who controlled the times had a power way beyond their rank.

The Bush House canteen was a wonderful place. Actors and guests would stay for lunch because it was cheap and cheerful. Producers and studio managers would gather to gossip. There were no privileged tables. On a busy day tables would be shared by newsreaders, senior managers and secretaries often having to raise voices against the babble of dozens of languages.

The canteen only became quieter after an intercom announcement warned the LSE students who'd crept in for a cheap lunch that their lectures were about to start.

Chris Faram

Spilling off the Reel

I have two abiding memories of Bush House – apart from the camaraderie, which was terrific.

The first is of the long night shift (22:00—09:00), which was sometimes quite busy and sometimes fairly quiet. Some of the recording studios we used were high up with windows that opened onto the Strand. On a quiet night, we would often liven things up by opening the windows and moving a couple of loudspeakers to face out of the window. We would then entertain any late-night revellers by playing a tape of the *1812 Overture* at high volume.

I also remember tapes that were wound tightly onto a single-sided core, so there was no supporting flange to prevent the tape from spilling off the reel. This meant you had to handle them very carefully.

Anyone who has been to Bush House will know the massive staircase that winds up from the ground to the top floor. So you can imagine the scene as a studio manger trots up the stairs carrying one of these tapes on a spindle ready for transmission. The tape spindle slips out of his hand and he manages to grab a piece of flying tape. The rest of the spindle rolls away down the stairs unwinding as it goes, leaving the studio manager holding the beginning of the tape. This is about 10 minutes before transmission.

Various people come out to help, going down the stairs and trying to straighten out the tape. One of the recording engineers cuts the tape so that the first five minutes or so can be wound onto a spool ready for transmission. While this is being done, the others are desperately trying to wind up the rest of the tape and get it onto a second spool, so that it can be cued in when the first spool runs out. They did, in fact, succeed, managing to load the spool onto the second tape machine. The transmission wasn't exactly seamless but it was better than 15 minutes of silence.

John Gardner

Value for Money

Value-for-money surveys are nothing new to the BBC. In 1987 I was instructed to show a value-for-money consultant, employed presumably at great expense, around our drama studio. He looked at it with deep suspicion. "It's very *big*, isn't it?" he said. "Most studios I've seen at Bush House are much smaller than this." I patiently explained that different parts of the studio gave us different acoustics, which were necessary to help an audience picture the narrative flow of a play. "If we were recording an echoey scene in a church, we'd use this bare-walled part of the studio, whereas if we wanted a deadish acoustic for exterior scenes, we'd use the felt-padded, curtained-off area." He nodded slowly, but seemed dissatisfied. "You mean, while you are using the curtained-off area, here, for an exterior scene, this large expanse of the walled area remains unoccupied?" I acknowledged that this was, indeed, sadly, the case. "It's an awful waste of space, isn't it?" he replied, disapprovingly. And then, struck by a sudden brainwave, asked me, in all seriousness, "Why don't you record two scenes at the same time?"

Gordon House

BBC and Misfortune

Once in the 1970s, the Urdu Service got a letter of complaint. A villager claimed the BBC was to be blamed for a snake bite he had in his private parts. While he was squatting down to relieve himself in the morning behind a bush in a ruined building, a radio in a nearby house was playing the BBC Urdu Service. According to him, the flute music of the theme summoned the snake which bit him. He demanded damages from the BBC for his misfortune.

Priyath Liyanage

World Service Sanctuary

In recent years the most popular and respected manager at Bush House was Kari Blackburn. Kari personified the Bush House family ethic of wide knowledge linked to a great capacity to care. She was at ease in any part of the BBC, but her love was Africa, and she always wished to become the head of the Africa Services at Bush House, emulating Dorothy Grenfill-Williams. This Kari achieved.

One morning Kari was seen to look very tired, exhausted even, and lacking her usual bounce and twinkle. It transpired that she had been at Heathrow all night, battling the immigration authorities. For eighteen months she had been trying to get a female producer from Mogadishu into the ranks of the Somali Service in Bush House. The service needed another female voice and point of view. Kari had selected the lady, and there the problems began. She needed to leave Somalia safely, with her family; she needed to get a visa at the British Embassy in Addis Ababa, and wasn't having any luck. Just when it seemed intractable, a new British Ambassador arrived in the Ethiopian capital – Bob Dewar, another true public servant. The paperwork was at last done, and the lady, with just two of her children, were granted their visas and were flying to Heathrow.

Kari knew the war was not won yet. She went to the airport, hours ahead of time. With her she had all the paperwork one would ever need: the contract from the BBC, professional and personal guarantees that the lady would be financed, and so on. By the time the plane landed Kari had made a pleasant nuisance of herself and was situated outside the chief immigration officer's door. Her new member of staff and the exhausted children were eventually allowed through. How many managers would have gone to Heathrow at night, not to greet their own children back from a skiing trip, but to help this small and worried family?

They were taken by taxi to a haven which used to exist in those days. One must not be starry-eyed about the past, but Beaumont House was a small BBC hostel in Prince's Square: truly a sanctuary, so useful and cost-effective. Hundreds of new recruits to the language services, many of them new to London and exhausted after getting away from horrible regimes, came to Beaumont over the years. What a statement of welcome and worth that was, to be cared for so well and to immediately feel part of the World Service family.

Over the next couple of weeks the lady was shown how to open a bank account, how to get a tube pass (Kari accompanied her on the first journey, there and back), how to apply for school places, where to buy suitable food, how to register with a doctor, and so on. And thus, into the Somali Service, greeted by tea and cakes, given a desk – and the freedom at last to be a real journalist.

This is just one story among hundreds which have been told about Kari, and this is why so many of us shed bitter tears at her untimely death a few years later.

Barry Langridge

"I Used to Be an Insomniac Until…"

My favourite listener's letter was from a Norwegian lady who wrote: "Dear Mr House. Thank you so much for those intellectually challenging plays you produce for us on Play of the Week. I used to be an insomniac until I started listening to your dramas. Keep up the good work!"

Gordon House

Ghostly Appearance

Somewhere in Bush House there is an Italian language service producer who, as part of his redundancy package a decade ago, was allowed to keep his office, so he comes in every day. A myth, I fear, but I'd love this to be true. Someone once nudged me in a lift nodding towards a departing figure, whispering "That's the Italian producer…"

Kirsty Cockburn

Long, Legg, Butt, Ruff, Short, Willey

In the early 1980s the main newsroom programme for correspondents' despatches was called Radio Newsreel, a progenitor of Newsdesk, which has since morphed into World Briefing. The editor's final job before the studio producer went into the studio was to confirm the running order by calling out the correspondents' names in sequence. One never to be forgotten day the order was "Long, Legg, Butt, Ruff, Short, Willey". Great correspondents. Great days. We shall not see their like again.

Chris Moore

Seeking Promotion

Back in the late 1970s, a journalist in the newsroom applied to become a chief subeditor. At his appointments board meeting, the personnel officer tactlessly noted that he had unsuccessfully sought promotion on 11 previous occasions. "Aren't you embarrassed by this?" asked the personnel officer. "No," replied the candidate, "but I thought you should be." He got the job.

Ian Richardson

Three Rules of Broadcasting

I remember the first three golden rules that Mr Rentoul gave me when he accepted me for the job. He made me write a test piece, read it underarm and then said three things. First, everywhere you put a comma, you put a full stop now because this is radio. Second, whatever your political beliefs and whatever your own ideas, leave them outside on the hanger with your coat when you come into the studio. And thirdly, don't sit down at a clean table in the canteen because it's just been wiped with a smelly rag. These were the first rules of broadcasting that I learned.

Peter Pallai

Iron Rules?

The Bush newsroom always insisted on two sources for a story – an iron rule. A fully fledged BBC staff reporter usually counted as two sources. Other single sources could be Reuters or AP – or a BBC language service stringer.

Often, one had an excruciating wait as a language service stringer reported from a remote spot where there were no other sources. The story was strong and good. We knew our reporter, we knew he had great contacts and we trusted them. Still the newsroom hung fire. This one source must be backed by a second.

We knew what to do. We rang the stringer and asked him to report as the local Reuters man – which they were – or as the local RFI man – which they also were. Two sources – no, three! The newsroom at last went with the story, appending, in its meticulous way, at the foot of the copy the code which meant local stringer, Reuters and RFI.

Barry Langridge

Calling Newfoundland

This goes back to the early 1970s when there was a programme titled Calling Newfoundland, presented by a very thin lady. She came into the control room one night asking, "Can anyone play the piano?" I said that I could a bit. "Well, can you come to the studio now? Because there is an opera singer form Newfoundland visiting here and I want her to sing in my programme and there's no one to play." Amidst protests that I would not be up to this, I was almost dragged to the studio where the young opera singing lady gave me some music. It was a bit too difficult for me to sight-read but I managed to plonk and plink a few notes at approximately the right time, and the young lady sang to it, bravely and beautifully. I escaped back to the control room to be told that it couldn't be used because I was not a member of the Musicians' Union. I replied that actually I was a member of that union – I was in a band but not as a pianist. They told me I would have to be paid for it to be OK, but there was no budget, so I never got my three minutes of fame.

Colin Neal

The Taliban on the Wavering Line

"Hello, is that the BBC Pashto Service?" Safia Haleem said that this was so – she knew from the use of a satphone and the tone of the speaker that this would be the Taliban. "Our commander wishes to speak to the BBC. We have the questions you must ask him. Please pass me to your superior." "There is no-one superior to me," said Safia. "No, no, kindly pass me quickly to the head of the BBC Pashto Service." "I am the head of the BBC Pashto Service."

There was silence on the wavering line. "Then kindly pass me to a male producer; the commander will not talk to you." "If your commander wishes to be interviewed by the BBC Pashto Service he will have to be interviewed by me or by no one at all." Silence. Then: "We will get back to you. Here are the questions." "We do not accept that the person to be interviewed should give the questions. We form the questions and we ask them during the interview."

A very long pause. "We will get back to you."

Barry Langridge

Chapter Three

History Live: "Would You Lend Us the Commando Brigade?"

The Oxfam of the Word

Bush House provided a window on the world to those deprived of the 20th century's light by the Nazis and the Communists. Imagine the depth of darkness if those two creeds, the most powerful of that era, had prevailed. For most of the last century Bush House lived up to the title bestowed upon it by a distinguished journalist of his day, "the Oxfam of the word".

Hugh Lunghi

Broadcasts to Make You Fit

During one of the ceasefires of civil war in Sri Lanka, a man came to Bush House and wanted to see someone from the Sinhala Service. When we met him, he said that he was so thrilled to see us. At that time, Tamil Tigers were ruling the northern territories of Sri Lanka. The government banned many goods from being taken across as the rebels were using them for military purposes. Among the banned items were batteries, which were used by the rebels to trigger landmines. There was no electricity in the area as the national grid was blown up by the rebels. The man who came to Bush House told us that all the people in his village listened to the BBC every day. They connected a radio to a bicycle dynamo and got a youngster to paddle it for half an hour. Everyone gathered around the stationary bicycle to listen to us. He was in tears that he could finally see us after becoming an asylum seeker in Britain.

Priyath Liyanage

Declaring Latvian Independence

An occasion which really stayed with me was in the late 1990s, when the Republic of Latvia decided to declare its independence. Lithuania had already done it, so it was number two among the Baltic states, but I thought I should go there. There was to be a vote in the parliament. They had no direct-dial phone, so I secured the one phone which had a link out to Poland and got my fix to listen to the debate in Latvian. When the vote came, he rushed through to me and inserted the numbers in my script, which was filed straight down the line to the Bush House newsroom so that they could get it into their next world news.

My job done, I went out and suddenly an MP rushed out from the parliament building, got up on a podium and said something very excitedly in Latvian. Then the whole crowd started shouting, "BBC, BBC!" I asked someone, "What are they saying?" And they told me: "The MP has heard the BBC World News – it's been announced that Latvia has declared its independence, so now we know it is true." A wonderful vindication of the World Service.

Bridget Kendall

The Last Mandarin Broadcast

I still remember our special transmission, the last Mandarin broadcast – that was a really emotional moment. Not just for the producers and my colleagues involved in the service, but also for all those listeners who have been with us all this time.

We received a lot of very supportive and comforting messages, either emails or even voice recordings. They all said that it was a very sad moment for them. Just after the transmission, immediately after we finished, one of the presenters actually burst into tears. The feeling was so strong I was almost overtaken by it, actually, and had to make an effort not to cry in front of my colleagues. It was quite hard.

Raymond Li

Unexpected Compliment

I interviewed Stokely Carmichael in New York in the early 1990s, when he was known as Kwame Ture and ran the All-African People's Revolutionary Party. After we'd finished recording, he said off the tape that when he had been in Guinea, where he had lived in exile, he had never missed the World Service classical music request programme The Pleasure's Yours presented by Gordon Clyde. Some years later, I met Gordon by chance and told him of Stokely's enthusiasm for his radio show – he was knocked out by the compliment.

Mike Popham

"It Would Be Wiser for You not to Visit Pakistan"

When I came back to the BBC in March 1971, Pakistan was going through its gravest crisis. This was brought about by the refusal of the West Pakistani rulers to accept the results of the general election held towards the end of 1970. In this election the Awami League Party headed by Sheikh Mujibur Rahaman had completely swept the board in the eastern part of the country. Rather than accept Mujibur Rahaman as the country's Prime Minister, its military rulers began a series of negotiations with him. But the talks ran into the sands and the government made the fateful decision to send the army to East Pakistan. As a result the atmosphere became highly charged not only in Pakistan but also among the Pakistani diaspora in Britain.

Most of my colleagues in the Urdu Section were backing the military action, so they felt that I was betraying Pakistan. Then there was the question of my audience. Because of my regular contributions to Pakistani television current affairs programmes, people knew me by sight. We received many abusive letters from our listeners in those days, along the lines of "You are talking nonsense, everything is OK." One letter, personally addressed to me, said: "It would be wiser for you not to visit Pakistan."

Throughout this traumatic period, the BBC tried to report events as truthfully as was possible in the very difficult situation created by the expulsion of the entire foreign media from East Pakistan. The BBC's version of events stood in sharp contrast to the one put out by the Pakistani media. With the surrender of the Pakistani army to the Indians and the emergence of Bangladesh as a sovereign nation, the people of Pakistan realised they had been bamboozled by their own media, while the BBC had been giving a true picture of the situation in East Pakistan. The much maligned BBC became popular as never before. After the army surrendered, I went to Pakistan but was very careful not to reveal my identity. Still, they recognised me and, to my great surprise, some officials at the airport came out of their room and greeted me very warmly. This experience was repeated throughout my stay there, wherever I went. Later, I did a programme on Pakistanis stranded in Bangladesh; a visit to their camp in Dhaka was a very moving experience. Our audience went up sharply around that time – everyone, from ministers to taxi drivers, was listening to the BBC Urdu service.

Viqar Ahmad

Bhutto's Hanging

I remember the night of the 3rd of April 1979. I did my story about Zulfiqar Ali Bhutto's hanging for my paper, the *Daily Sun*. It was all based on unofficial sources, speculations and rumours, because the authorities were not prepared to say anything about it. Even the close relatives of Bhutto refused to speak on the subject. I was warned that I should be very careful with the story. Anything irresponsible might land the paper as well as me in trouble.

The story was given a front page treatment with a banner lead, "Bhutto to be hanged this morning?" No other paper in Karachi carried the story in its morning edition. I was bewildered and waited in the office very impatiently for the BBC morning transmission, Jehanuman, but when I found that the story was not carried by them, I panicked, because that meant that Bhutto was not hanged and I could be taken to task for rumour mongering. So I went home with a long face, took two sleeping pills and went to bed. When I woke up, a special supplement of the *Daily Jang* was out with the story, after it was covered by the BBC Urdu Service. That was the credibility of the BBC: if an event of some importance had taken place, people expected it to include it in its news. If it was not there it meant that the event had not taken place or was not as important as it was shown to be by the local media.

Ali Ahmed Khan

Why Are We Interviewing Him?

Before the 1976 election in Pakistan, there was a big opposition movement against Zulfiqar Ali Bhutto, led by Air Marshal Asghar Khan. He came to London on one occasion and it was suggested that the Urdu Service should interview him. But the question was, why are we interviewing him? This was debated, and we did eventually do an interview with him – not just because he was here on a visit but because we really wanted to talk to him.

Another example was when I went to Pakistan as a correspondent and there was a similar movement against General Zia-ul-Haq. People were somehow able to manage to have rallies here and there – the word went around but, of course, none of this would be advertised by the Pakistani media. So people would come up to me and say, "We're having a big rally tomorrow. Can you put this on your programme?" The reply had to be, "Well, I'm very sorry but the BBC is a news organisation. If something is newsworthy then we'll report it, but we're not actually a notice board for political events in Pakistan." And I think people sometimes found that difficult, saying, "Oh, but you're being unfair to us. We need a voice."

Towyn Mason

Talking Across the River Neelum

People in divided Kashmir, Indian and Pakistani Kashmir, were talking to each other across the river Neelum – they would gather on the banks and shout across to each other, or they would send messages in bottles. We thought that there was something the BBC could do, so we set up these makeshift studios in Sinega and Muzzafarabad, where people actually saw each other for the first time in 20, 25 years: fathers, sons, mothers, sisters. I believe only the BBC could have done that, because we had resources in both places, a strong presence and a great reputation in both parts of Kashmir. It was a very big moment for the Urdu Service, which itself became news, having united these people who had been divided.

Waheed Mirza

Bharat Broadcasting Corporation

We were all aware of the pressure from the Pakistani government, and I remember when I went to West Pakistan I was shown a letter which said about five different things about the BBC. One of them was about the Bharat Broadcasting Corporation. Another, which I always remember, if you'll excuse a rather vulgar phrase, referred to the British Bullshit Corporation. So we knew that the Pakistani government was putting pressure on the BBC, we knew also that there were sections of the British government, particularly the High Commission in Pakistan, which thought we were biased, but we didn't suffer for this in the same way as our correspondents on the ground did.

Mark Tully

Special Assignment

During the war between China and India in 1962, Tunku Abdul Rahman, the Chief Minister of Malaysia, issued a statement that he would offer his blood for the jawans (soldiers) of India. And the head of the Commonwealth, Britain, the BBC didn't say a word. I was a little upset, so I did satyagraha, just sat down and didn't do anything. Then my programme organiser came and asked, "What are you doing today?" I said, "Nothing, I don't feel like doing anything." "Why?" I said, "Look, Tunku Rahman of Malaysia is offering blood for Indian soldiers and you people, the head of the Commonwealth, you have not even uttered a word." So after an hour, he came back and said, "You've got a special assignment. Every day you have to write a talk on this Sino-Indian war." In a few days' time, there was a ceasefire, so I thought, "Good gracious, now I'm free and I don't have to write again" (it gets boring after a while). But my programme organiser said, "No, you can't trust these Chinese, they may resume, so you keep on writing."

Mahendra Kaul

"Do You Ever Listen to the BBC Urdu Service?"

One of the best stories that I remember is from the time when I started following the BBC Urdu Service as a magazine editor in Karachi. I asked one of my young staffers, "Do you ever listen to the Urdu Service?" She laughed and said, "That's like asking me if I've ever worn a sari."

Aamer Ahmed Khan

Lifting the Lid off Totalitarianism

When I came to work in Bush House the war had ended a bare ten years ago. One murderous totalitarian system, Nazism, had been destroyed. Another was very much alive and kicking. Hitler was dead; Stalin, his one-time ally, alive but mad, raving about the doctors' plot to assassinate him, as he prepared to engulf his own people in another Holocaust. Both systems were closed societies; in any case, the media worldwide was pathetically small during the first half of the century. The BBC, through is objectivity during the war, had lifted the lid off Hitler's propaganda.

The low-key cold war Stalin had waged against his allies, the US and Britain, even during the conflict with the common Nazi enemy, was by now a fully blown anti-imperialist propaganda war for Moscow. Russia's neighbours, the countries of eastern Europe, were drowning under the blood tide of Stalin's puppet communist regimes.

Bush House with its cosmopolitan staff, many exiles from Stalin's terror, helped to present the evidence which showed how the anti-communist uprisings (East Berlin in 1953, Poland in 1953 and 1956, Hungary in 1956, Czechoslovakia 1968), although crushed by Moscow, in the event turned out to be two steps forward and only one step back. They led eventually to the collapse of the Soviet system and were by far the most important historical events of those decades.

Hugh Lunghi

As Truthful as Reasonably Possible

It is remarkable how the BBC built up a reputation for truthfulness and reliability – not only during the war, but long after. The Nazis prohibited short-wave radios not because they were afraid of the effect of British "propaganda" broadcasts, but of the effect of straight news bulletins. It is a humbling thought that people in occupied Europe, and later in the Soviet sphere, risked imprisonment and sometimes death in order to find out what was going on in the world. I spoke to many people after the war, in Germany and in Czechoslovakia, and was invariably told that the BBC was far more popular than the lavishly endowed American-sponsored stations like The Voice of America and Radio Free Europe. While I believe this reputation to be justified, and while I am proud that my work may have contributed to it, honesty compels me to admit that the truthfulness of BBC news bulletins was not quite a hundred per cent. We were far more frank with our audiences than any other government in wartime – but even so, not completely. I remember that, at the height of the U-boat battle, we did not always acknowledge the full extent of our losses, although, of course, it can be claimed that this was done to keep the enemy guessing. Exaggerated figures of enemy aircraft shot down during the Battle of Britain, on the other hand, were probably due to the fact that more than one RAF fighter pilot – in good faith – claimed the destruction of the same German machine. On balance, we are entitled to be proud to have been as truthful as we were.

Ewald Osers

Keeping the Lights on

When the BBC installs a new FM facility in Africa, it does so in a partnership involving a local broadcaster, often the state broadcaster. This is all launched with publicity and a party. From the BBC's point of view there is an almost automatic increase in the local urban audience because FM is, of course, held to be far superior to our short-wave signal.

At the launch party in Freetown, the capital of Sierra Leone, there were interesting visitors: a small group of tired-looking Europeans. "We are here to beg you never to cut short-wave services to this part of the world," they said.

When asked what proof they had that short-wave radio was still effective, their leader said: "We help to run a large hospital in Liberia, away from the towns. Our electrical supply is almost always off, and we have generators, which are expensive. At night the wards are in darkness but we always keep the lights on along our verandas. It has little to do with the patients, it is to serve dozens of children who know the lights will be on, so they travel to us to read their books and do their homework. They sit very quietly, sometimes with their parents, and we sit with them and play the BBC World Service on our short-wave radio, which we have rigged to loudspeakers."

We made a note to take this back to the BBC cost-cutters and heads of strategy – of which there were many, and none of them ever seemed to have ventured further abroad than Greece. When we thanked the visitors for coming all this way they said, "We are the grateful ones. Focus on Africa and Newshour and Outlook are precious to us. We know the names of all the presenters. The staff, the kids and the patients wait for them each evening. Please, please keep sending the short-wave signal in. We will keep the lights going so long as you keep broadcasting your wonderful material."

Barry Langridge

"A Foreigner in My Bed!"

On the morning of the 2nd of January 1993 I was finishing a night shift, having a coffee in the Bush House canteen before going home and chatting with colleagues who had just come in to start their day. A friend from the Slovak Service, a lively and charming woman, joined our table. At one point she looked at us and said with a bright smile, "Do you know what happened to me this morning? I woke up, and there was a foreigner in my bed!" We laughed, a little puzzled. Then I remembered meeting her husband once: he was a Czech. And I also remembered that morning's news: Czechoslovakia had split in two the previous day.

Xavier Kreiss

Fairness, Balance and Accuracy

After the massacres in Africa known as the Great Lakes refugee crisis, Benny Ammar – then the head of the region – asked the BBC to set up a new service for Rwanda and Burundi. It became an instant hit, attracting huge audiences desperate for accurate news.

Soon the World Service was welcomed into both countries for FM partnerships. The BBC offered training to local journalists. This was snapped up. However, when the first course in radio techniques of interviewing was complete, and it was time for the public presentation of certificates to the course members, a question was asked – a question which might have been asked in so many parts of the world after such a course.

In front of the BBC delegation, the Minister of Information and the director-general of Rwandan broadcasting, a tall young woman was pushed to the front to give the thanks of the course members. She did this nicely, in good English. Then she hesitated, and looked at her mates, who all nodded at her.

"Ladies and gentlemen, we are all grateful to have learnt the basics of fairness, balance and accuracy in interviewing officials and politicians. But we all feel that these new skills will be of no use to us unless our editors and bosses and even our politicians are trained in the same skills. When you leave this place, there will be absolutely no possibility of any of us being able to use these things. Yet we thank you for your intentions."

There was a dreadful silence. Then someone proposed the health of the Rwandan Republic, and soft drinks were taken.

Barry Langridge

I Dreaded Pressing the Wrong Switch

Walter Ulbricht, the unpopular East German leader, despite being a hard-line communist, reinstated the teaching of English in the GDR: he might not like what he felt the language stood for, but his officials needed it. In July 1973 he suffered a stroke. The German Service prepared an obituary tape, and for a week or so studio managers had to take it to every German transmission in case news of his death came through while the programme was on air. The typical 15-minute transmission would consist of a 10-minute live news bulletin followed by a five-minute pre-recorded programme. I had just finished my training and was being let loose on simpler transmissions, but one tape box looks much like another, and I dreaded pressing the wrong switch and announcing Ulbricht's death to a surprised world.

Fast-forward to East Berlin in September 1989. By then I was working for the BBC English by Radio and Television, and we had been developing links with radio and television stations as well as publishers and English language teacher groups in the Soviet Union and eastern Europe. On a trip to Germany, I had the strange experience of standing on the eastern side of the Brandenburg gate, but being unable to go through to visit a friend in West Berlin.

We'd had contacts with East German television, and a few years earlier Bernd Dammasch, from the GDR Educational Department, had visited London. In an airless hospitality room in Centre Block we watched some of his programmes and showed Mr Dammasch one from our own TV series Follow Me, which had been directed by Ian McNaughton (who had previously worked on Monty Python) and provided a very different approach to learning. There were, though, similarities: Follow Me was very much aimed at those who had missed out on learning English the first time around.

I'd almost forgotten the meeting and was surprised to be greeted by a three-man reception committee once I'd navigated the unwelcoming immigration counters at East Berlin's Schönefeld airport. "Herr Dammasch remembers with great pleasure meeting you and is looking forward to seeing you again." While I was discussing the language they planned to use in their next TV series, the Hungarian government was letting in East German refugees. Two months later the Berlin Wall was opened, and soon East Germany ceased to exist.

Hamish Norbrook

Golden Era Features

My introduction to the BBC was through a marvellous book written by a journalist who was associated with the BBC Hindustani Service in the days of the Second World War. It contained London letters broadcast during that period. Very few people in the Indian subcontinent were regular listeners of the BBC at that time. Those who could afford it used large car battery radio sets or home made ones, which could receive only local radio broadcasts. I was ten years old when I made such a set with discarded telephone receiver cans. I heard the shocking news of Gandhi's assassination on the 30th of January 1948 on that set.

I joined the Urdu Service in 1983. David Page, who was heading the service, used my journalistic contacts with the Asian community in Europe and threw a challenge to me in March 1983 to collect material for a series on Asians in Europe. This opened a new chapter in the journalistic coverage of the issues in which subcontinent listeners were interested, expanding the horizon of the service beyond the UK and the Indian subcontinent. It was further widened when I did a long series on the newly independent former Soviet Republics in Central Asia in 1992.

That was a golden era of extremely interesting, informative and popular feature programmes and series aimed at different groups. The live coverage of the first Gulf War by CNN created a myth that broadcasting institutions have to focus mainly on rolling news and current affairs. As some of our programmes became victims of this myth, the Urdu Service lost a great number of listeners. No doubt there were other contributing factors, including the disappearance of short-wave radio sets in the subcontinent, the proliferation of TV channels and the growing independence of the media.

To arrest the decrease in listenership, the crutches of an FM radio network were adopted. The outsourced service is listened to through FM radios but the quality and content of its programmes have suffered a great deal. It appears that their format style and language are tailored to the needs of the short and racy format of FM radios. You can call it a new digital broadcasting era, but the fact is that the old Urdu Service, which reigned over the minds and the hearts of the millions in the subcontinent and beyond for the past 70 years, has disappeared.

Asaf Jilani

Shaheen Club

I joined the Urdu Section in 1972 and was retired 24 years later. You can call this the era of mass listening. I personally saw people going to their rooftops or driving their cars out of town for the sake of getting a better and clearer signal. One simple reason was their thirst for reliable, impartial and credible news. But the listeners back home were not glued to solid news and views – they were listening to features or non-current affairs programmes as well in millions.

The first programme I was asked to produce was the listeners' letters slot called Anjuman, where only the BBC and its programmes were discussed. We turned it into a family show and talked about the listeners, too. The number of letters we were receiving shot up from four thousand to more than 40 thousand a year. After that, in 1975, I suggested to start a weekly programme about rare Urdu books, which were published during the 19th century and are well preserved here in the India Office Library. I was granted 12 weeks to discuss this treasure, and the programme got so popular that it went on for 120 weeks.

Another milestone which contributed to the title of mass listening given to this period was our children's programme called Shaheen Club, a 15-minute slot of jokes and laughter. The entire populations of Indian towns were listening to it regularly. A team of Pakistan Air Force pilots visiting the UK once dropped in Bush House to meet the main character of the show, Siddhu Bhai.

We had women's programmes, cultural and literary programmes, Science and Space, Questions and Answers, Sports Round-up, Life in Britain – these are some of the gems of the Urdu Service. Some people called the BBC a news organisation. We proved it to be wrong. We were successful in giving it a soft image, while winning the listeners' hearts. We developed a close relationship with them, so much so that when the main character of Shaheen Club, Siddhu Bhai had a stroke, listeners all over India and Pakistan prayed for him with such a devotion and wrote so many letters, which were passed on to him in the hospital, that he recovered within weeks – the doctors were amazed by his quick recovery. That was the magic of the BBC Urdu Service.

Raza Ali Abidi

Shah Sahib

I was very fortunate to join the BBC Urdu Service in 1984, when it was at the peak of its popularity. The names of its producers and broadcasters were household names in Pakistan. Although the BBC was known for its current affairs programmes, weekly features like Shaheen Club, which was meant for children, were equally popular among grown-ups.

When my children joined me in London in 1985, they asked me if I knew Siddhu Bhai, the late Mr Shah – we used to call him Shah Sahib – who played the main character in Shaheen Club. I told them that he was my colleague and a good friend, but they were not prepared to believe it. So I had to invite him to my place and my children prepared halwa for the occasion – it's a sweet dish, and Siddhu Bhai, in Shaheen Club, was very fond of it. Normally Shah Sahib was not allowed to take sugar in tea or coffee as he was a diabetic. Once a prominent politician from Pakistan visited Bush House and requested a meeting with Siddhu Bhai, which I arranged and the visitor was grateful for that.

Ali Ahmed Khan

Grey Building

Approaching the Ministry of Information in Luanda, we didn't think we would get much joy out of our discussions with the Angolan government. Perhaps understandably, they were very jumpy about radio – which they themselves had used to great effect in their long and vicious civil war.

We had been well briefed by the head of our Portuguese Service, who was with us. Angolan by birth, he knew that our broadcasts here and in Mozambique were very closely monitored, but he felt that times were changing and was hopeful that we might get some sort of partnership deal with the state broadcaster, with our going on FM in Luanda. Perhaps they might agree that we run our English programmes if not yet Portuguese – it was a compromise which we were prepared for.

Jao had worked hard towards the meeting, so I was astonished when he stood in front of the grim pile of the Ministry and said that he might not come in. He didn't want to, but we insisted that it was important that he be there. It was a satisfactory meting but with no real breakthrough. Our head of the Portuguese Service made few contributions and was clearly ill at ease throughout. Later that evening, over beers, he told us why.

As a young man he had won a scholarship to study in Cuba. Just as he was going back, expecting a welcome and various government posts, there was a regime change in Luanda. When he arrived home he was arrested by the suspicious authorities. Jao did survive, but only after spells of torture in the basements of the Ministry of Information – that same grey building we had visited that morning.

Barry Langridge

The Nature of Burmese Tyranny

In the summer of 1988 I was sent by the BBC Eastern Service to Burma with a tourist visa because General Ne Win, the man who had ruled Burma in his slightly crazy, idiosyncratic fashion since 1962, said there would be a party congress not after the usual five year affair, but after two and a bit years.

The night I got there he went on television and said he was going to resign, that there would be multi-party politics. That led to extraordinary events, nationwide protests which were eventually to come to very abrupt end in September 1988 with a massacre in which they gunned down hundreds if not thousands of innocent Burmese people. Such is the nature of Burmese tyranny that one could not go in and do proper reporting. Everything was very cloak-and-dagger. So I went in with a tourist visa, but shortly after I got there Ne Win resigned and the whole anti-government protest started.

All of the workers in my hotel were on the side of freedom, freedom of expression, freedom of information. As the only western journalist there I was given free phone lines to London whenever I wanted. I was given free taxi rides. I was taken wherever I wanted to. I felt as if the whole of Burma were really my news sources and were helping me. It was a wonderfully liberating feeling for a young BBC cub reporter.

Chris Gunness

Attacks and Demonstrations

It was great fun going into Indian villages and being with villagers when they listened to radio. A friend of mine always tells a story of going into a village with me during an election and asking the villagers who is winning. Someone told him: "The BBC hasn't said yet, so I don't know."

I remember a time in Pakistan in the days of Zulfikar Ali Bhutto, when the government was very angry with the BBC during the movement against him. As I was reporting his parliamentary speech in Islamabad, I found the whole speech was an attack on me and on the BBC. I didn't know what was going to happen to me, whether I was going to be arrested, carted out of the building, chucked out of Pakistan, but at the end Bhutto screamed to the top of his voice: "We are generous nation and we will not do anything to him." So I left and found taxi driver sitting outside, who said, "My ears were burning when I heard that speech" – he was able to hear it on the radio in his cab.

There was a time when we had protests outside the BBC office for a whole week, because someone had interviewed a Sikh leader in London, who had said that after the army attack on the Golden Temple it was likely that Mrs Gandhi would be killed. So we had a week of demonstrations which ended with people chucking stones through the window of my flat and trying to climb over the fence and get into the flat and the office above.

Mark Tully

Mr Big Foot

One cross often carried by the World Service staff, and in particular by the regular stringers abroad who file day after day from difficult places, is the tendency of rather inflated people from the BBC News who often get the story late from our stringers and then rush to the spot and "uncover" or "discover" the story, squashing the doughty local with their big feet. This was felt very heavily in the World Service, and those who did not do it – Lyse Doucet, Mark Tully, several others – were admired.

The most famous example of this occurred when one of these types arrived in Afghanistan to announce that he had "liberated" Kabul. This caused huge mirth. The

Pashto and Persian Services had been reporting from the capital for weeks, and a British reporter, William Reeve, had almost been killed by a bomb which had blown his studio door apart.

Thus it was with the Darfur story, when the person who had been to the hell of the swelling refugee camps, and was already filing for the Arabic Service, Focus on Africa, the Swahilis and the Bush House newsroom, suddenly found she had to fight for a place on a relief plane out of Nairobi, because the squadrons had arrived from London – correspondents, researchers and technicians with silvery boxes full of TV equipment. All anxious to film the chaotic misery and get it back for the Ten O'Clock News.

When our Portuguese stringer in Mozambique began to file on a sudden flooding in her country, she also found herself big-footed by people from London – several days late but not a dollar short. There were few flights over the vast flooded plane, so the stronger and more monied BBC types got their seats in relief helicopters – and managed to take wonderful shots of misery; of bags of rice being thrown down to plucking hands and people sitting in trees (their coup was to find a lady actually having her baby in a tree). But these carpetbaggers had forgotten one thing: none of them knew Portuguese nor any of the local languages; they didn't really know which river and which coast or which region they were actually looking at, so they had to check everything back at Maputo with the patient stringer who had broken the story and had been left at the helipad.

Surprisingly, this valiant local never got a mention, and certainly not a shot, on Ten O'Clock News that night, nor on Breakfast or on Today the next morning. However, there is a God. When a young reporter happened to be on site for some nastiness in Nepal, he witnessed a very satisfying scene. He and Mark Tully, who had come up from Delhi, had been working on the story for two days, with Mark very kindly letting the young man do some filing, when everybody really wanted only him. There was a curfew, but we had been allowed to travel around with an armed guard, because Mark's tough and experienced local stringer Kedar Man Singh was known and respected and had got the permissions.

After the curfew was lifted, we saw to our dismay a particularly tough and tactless big-footer barge into our hotel dining-room, followed by two men with those ominous shiny metallic cases. The big-footer strode up to our table. "Hi Mark, what's going on?" Mark said that our colleagues were here, the young man from London and our local correspondent, Mr Kedar Man Singh.

The big-footer pulled out of his breast pocket a thick set of travel documents. "Hi. Kedar, is it? Can you get us out of here by Friday?" It was a horrid moment. Mark, who never swore, leapt to his feet and grabbed the docket. "He is our colleague, our correspondent! Without him here, we and you are nothing. Confirm your own ruddy tickets!" Mark threw the stuff onto the floor. "And go and sit at another table, will you!"

Barry Langridge

Thin Aerogramme

I remember a blue letter coming from Kabul, this thin aerogramme, written by a woman. It said, "Why doesn't the international community send troops to Afghanistan?" She was asking for blue berets, United Nations soldiers, to be sent to her country.

This was one of my first jobs, and I thought, "It's such an important letter — maybe we can read it." And then I realised that any request like this would be seen as a joke, as something that would never ever happen, not only by the authorities but even by your own colleagues.

Najiba Kasraee

Accolade From Hungarian Radio

Mr Rentoul, once the head of the Hungarian Section, told me that Hungarian Radio sent a message to the BBC during the 1956 revolution, thanking the corporation for its honesty. Out of 11 western radio stations broadcasting in Hungarian, the BBC alone received that accolade from Hungarian Radio.

Peter Pallai

Signed by Sheikh

The BBC was called the sixth prayer in Afghanistan as it was a must to listen to the evening programme in Pashto. Instead of your chasing interviewees, they would call and tell you about this or that happening. It was a very interesting time.

I also remember the first few weeks after US special forces landed in the northern parts of Afghanistan and the Taliban in Kabul didn't know about that yet. I was on a night shift, we called them and asked: "Do you know that the Americans are already in Afghanistan?" And this commander told me he didn't believe it and then he said, "They're just fighting from above, let them come down to the ground, then we'll show them." A few days later we received a fax, it was written in Arabic, and the title of the sender was Sheikh. It wasn't signed "Bin Laden", but everyone knew that was his title. I think his idea was that we condemn the American attacks to show our solidarity with the Afghan Muslim brotherhood.

Najiba Kasraee

Post-Transmission Tea Parties

In 1982 the Falklands war ushered in a very traumatic period for the members of the then Latin American Service. Latin America had closed ranks behind Argentina almost to a man, and our relatives were tearfully questioning our commitment to the BBC during distressingly regular phone calls. Meanwhile, there were rumours that the Argentine staff in London would have their bank accounts frozen on UK government orders, so the tension was high.

In addition to all that, we had to crank up the journalism, which was being heavily scrutinised in both London and Buenos Aires. We were broadcasting a live current affairs programme and the stakes were high. Argentina was living under a ferocious military dictatorship and even then there was a famous cartoon in an Argentine paper where, after a particular battle around the Falklands, one guy whispers to another, "What did the BBC say?"

One night we got a phone call from a chaplain who was with the Argentine forces in the Falklands before the Royal Navy arrived. He phoned us up to say, "If you could see them, these are terrified boys that have been brought down from the mountains, please, please do something."

Broadcasters from Argentina held it together, of course, but then, coming off air, I remember them bursting into tears. Then the studio manager spread the news around Bush House about how difficult it was for us. And so people started arriving in the studio with cakes and coffees and they wouldn't talk much about the war. Little was said of any significance, but their presence in the studio, their warmth made every difference to us. As the war went on, their numbers gradually grew. Many enduring friendships were formed in these post-transmission tea parties. Our colleagues were there to make us feel better, to make us feel supported, and I can still get quite emotional about it because it was such a British thing to do. To come in not to make fuss, but simply to say, here we are – you are not alone.

Julia Zapata

Tears on Both Ends of the Phone

One of my memories is of being in Bush House on the day the Falklands war was declared. I was still working in Overseas Administration and was hurriedly seconded to Calling the Falklands, just for one day, to field telephone calls from anxious friends and relatives of those living and working in the Falklands. It was an emotional day – lots of people in tears on both ends of the phone. I still remember taking a call from the Mayor of Crewkerne in Somerset, who was offering support to the Falkanders as the sheep on the islands had come from the stock originally bred in the town.

Caroline Dunton

"Would You Lend Us the Commando Brigade?"

Once we had the Israeli invasion of South Lebanon in 1982, which was terribly destructive, and at the same time Britain was fighting in the Falklands. So I sort of ran two wars simultaneously. One Friday afternoon my telephone rang – it was an Egyptian general who said, "I wish to compliment you on your coverage of both your war and our war," and then, "Would you lend us the commando brigade?"

Eric Bowman

Rumour and Fact

It was a salutary experience for all of us that when one of the correspondents in Vietnam, a very good one, who had been reporting on the fighting in the country, said in a throwaway line: "There were reports, not yet confirmed, that the South Vietnamese government was going to abandon a particular area in South Vietnam".

This report had being going around for ages, and no one had taken any notice of it, but the moment the BBC said it, everyone thought it must be true. Once the BBC mentioned it, even if only in passing, it was considered fact.

Ian Richardson

Farming Forecasts

Working for the BBC Monitoring Service during the Second World War, I don't recall having had any problems with the monitoring of news bulletins or political talks – that was just the language of newspapers. However, our intelligence customers were interested just as much, and maybe even more, in German broadcasts for farmers – these, it was explained, might be informative on food shortages, crop expectations and even the weather.

Ewald Osers

The Pakistani Sage

One of the greatest pleasures to be had in Bush House was to go down to the canteen for coffee and choose your table. It could be the Chinese staff, garnished with a Thai; it could be a conglomeration of trainers fresh back from Latin America; it could be a large and very loud table of Swahilis mixed with West Africans; it could be a quiet table of Indonesians sitting with the Burmese. Which to choose? Everybody was so friendly. Even Pakistanis sometimes sat with Hindus and Bengalis.

On one occasion I spotted a table of great wisdom and wit. There was the Turkish Service head, a senior Russian, the deputy head of the Ukrainian Service and an experienced Urdu senior producer.

I joined the table. For Pakistan and democracy it seemed to be exciting times; the military President Zia-ul-Haq had just perished in a plane crash, the Americans were demanding that there should be elections, and even as we spoke, the youthful Benazir Bhutto was announcing her intention to return to Pakistan and run for office. She had been educated at Oxbridge, she was beautiful, and she spoke movingly about democracy for her beleaguered nation. So I sat down, waiting to hear the good news.

"My friend," said the Urdu senior, Mr Ali Ahmed Khan. "I am sorry, but she will win and she will be useless." Useless! But hadn't her father been hanged by the military? "She will be unable to do anything. All she has is her name – her name and the Bhutto arrogance and the Pakistan People's Party. She is hated in Karachi and disliked in most of Punjab and therefore will be ignored by the army. She will be surrounded by the same old names." "But surely, the Americans..." "My friend," said the Pakistani sage. "Many westerners make the mistake of thinking that when people have been in opposition for a long time, they become clean. But corruption can be anywhere. When the opposition finally comes to power in Ukraine and in Russia, you will see the same thing. Turkey is the only hope, and, of course, the Burmese lady. Bhutto may return on her white charger, but for the poor in Pakistan it will be the same old shit." The what? That word, used in the Bush House canteen? The others all nodded. "I am sorry. But the same old shit!"

As it turned out, they were all correct. Since that day, quite a long time ago, it has, unfortunately, been the same old shit in Pakistan. I rose from the table. The central writers and the Radio 4 lot were at that exact time rhapsodising about Miss Bhutto and the shining future. Documentaries were being made about her time in exile. None of the producers, though, had checked with Bush House or spoken to Mr Ali Ahmed Khan.

As the World Service joins the Broadcasting House, our domestic colleagues could do worse than go to the canteen, be humble and sit quietly at a table made up of people like this.

Barry Langridge

Branded "Traitors"

The BBC Sinhala Service, with its thin budget and its six staff, has been at the centre of crises for much of its life. In Bush House it has fought the same battles as many small but important services, to handle repeated parings of its funds and to keep itself off the bottom of the various "priority lists" drawn up now and then. It has never been good for morale to know that you are always down there somewhere; but the service soldiered on.

However, its greatest battle has always been to prove, day after day, that it has been reporting fairly on the vicious recent history of Sri Lanka. Its huge success, in terms of audience proportions, has always made it an easy target for Tamil extremists on the one hand, and flag-waving politicians and generals on the other.

So the Sinhala Service has become used to be being branded "traitors" for not loyally reporting the war from one side only. Their critics in Colombo dutifully briefed UK delegations, Heads of Mission and even newly arrived English-stream BBC reporters, telling them that all would be well if it were not for the poisonous shrimp of the Sinhala Service and its partner-in-crime, the BBC Tamil Service. Rather shamefully, there have been BBC journalists, anxious for access, who have been almost seduced by all this.

Whenever BBC investigations were made, it was always found that the members of the service, despite sometimes intense personal pressures, were playing it straight. Not bland, not careful, but straight. Stalemates, claims of victorious battles or atrocities were always reported in the infuriatingly balanced BBC way.

It was a surprise, therefore, that we were granted access to a large number of FM relays across Sri Lanka. The radio stream on our frequency was a mixture of the main BBC English World Service output, interlarded with the programmes of the two troublesome services. Why was this permission granted? Was it because there would be embarrassment otherwise? Was it an expression of the local government's undertaking to promote free speech and its policy of supporting all kinds of links between the national media and the BBC?

There was another element here. In many parts of the world, especially as alternative and new media services have sprung up, the BBC audiences have shown resilience because people like to go back to the BBC after they have listened to a comfortable and reassuring local or state station. For example, when Al Jazeera began its Arabic Service it was said – and confirmed – that while listeners and viewers liked the use of Al Jazeera's phrases for Arabs fighting against Israel ("martyrs", "freedom fighters"), they would always check facts with the BBC, which continued to use our time-honoured measured phrases, such as "activists" or "militants".

At the end of the civil war in the north of Sri Lanka, with the smashing of the Liberation Tigers of Tamil Eelam's resistance and claims of atrocities on both sides, the Sinhala Service was under enormous pressure. News blackouts, a lack of witnesses, doubtful claims by the LTTE, bland statements by the government, an increasingly virulent criticism of the BBC, a huge relief and jubilation of the great majority of Sri Lankans – it was a testing time.

During a four-hour-long TV and radio performance, Commander of the Army, Sarath Fonseka, was asked what he made of "the BBC traitors". In the heat of his epic address he said that if he could extradite them from the UK he would bring them back to Colombo and try them for treason. However, the war hero overreached himself, as war heroes sometimes do. He stood for the office of President against the incumbent at the next election. After many wrangles, mutual accusations and a trial, Fonseka found himself in prison.

While incarcerated, he confessed that the tedium of the local radio services was relieved only by his ability to get the BBC, and especially the Sinhala Service, on his small FM radio. On which, one supposes, his pleas of innocence and of political chicanery were fairly reported, as were the counter-statements of the government.

Priyath Liyanage

"This Is What We Are Going to Do"

The fourth floor newsroom: normally the quiet hum of keyboard clicks, muted phone calls, intelligent thought and occasional beeps from the tannoy announcing an incoming piece from a correspondent. The date is the 11th of September 2001. The place suddenly erupts into pandemonium as journalists witness the first plane hitting the World Trade Centre on their TV monitors, which are dotted all over the newsroom.

After a minute or so, the senior duty editor that day, the person in charge of the newsroom, climbs onto her desk and shouts to everyone to calm down. "This is obviously a major story," she said. "And this is what we are going to do." This brief and rare moment of emotion over, the World Service's news machine cranks smoothly into action for live round-the-clock coverage.

Hugh Saxby

A Brotherly Dispute

In 2003, I was part of a team of BBC journalists sent to Iraq after the war that ended the regime of Saddam Hussein. The group included some of the most experienced correspondents, such as Barbara Plett, Claire Marshall and Stephen Sackur, the presenter of HARDtalk. Though we hardly knew each other, within a short time we stopped being mere colleagues and became friends. In Baghdad we lived in a villa that the BBC had rented, as the Palestine Hotel was increasingly targeted by soldiers still loyal to Hussein, who did not want to leave the capital.

I and Stephen Sackur shared a bedroom divided into two parts. Throughout our journey Stephen insisted, in a brotherly manner, that the youngest of the group should receive more attention. When there were only three bottles of water or a packet of biscuits to share, Stephen would turn to me and say, in an authoritative voice but with humor, "Here, Venuste, you're the youngest." I kept telling them that I was not the youngest, but they were convinced they had to protect me, despite one colleague reminding them that it was difficult to guess the age of an African. Had they believed him, I wouldn't have enjoyed that much privilege.

In April 2003, Stephen and I went to Hilla, a town not far from Babylon, where mass graves containing the remains of the victims of the 1991 repressions against Shiites were discovered. It was extremely hot, even for an African like myself. When we were down to our last bottle of water, Stephen, ever the gentleman, left it for me. I had to pretend that I had had enough because I could visibly see that he was thirsty. That was my way of paying back for his brotherly care.

The journey back was difficult too. It was an eight-hour drive to the Kuwait border. Halfway through, we stopped for lunch. We only had the food rations given to us by the British and American soldiers we had left behind. As usual, sharing was the rule, and good humor prevailed. The corn beef was very good – I guess anything would have been – but there was not enough for everyone. And then I sprung my surprise. I suggested that we give the remaining box to the oldest person among us. Since there was no consensus on who the oldest was, I said we should check our identity cards. After a brief investigation, I officially became the undisputed oldest man in the group. Stephen could not believe he was a year younger than me. True, he started working for the Beeb earlier than me. He has 25 years to his tally, against the 15 that I just clocked up at our iconic Bush House. So I still regard Stephen as my big brother. And soon we will be working together under the same roof in our new home, the New Broadcasting House.

Venuste Nshimiyimana

Bush House from an airship, taken on the photographer's 50th birthday in 1987
(Ian D. Richardson)

Lion guarding Bush House
(Emily Kasriel)

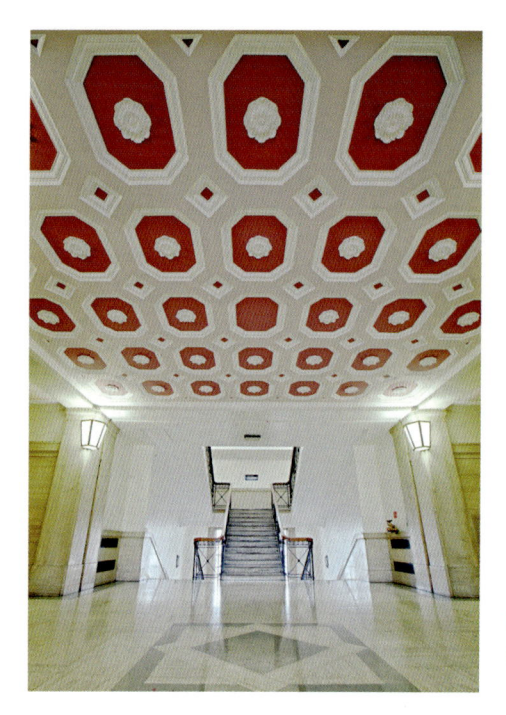

Entering Bush: lobby, Centre Block
(Orlando Gili)

Up the stairs, to where news is made
(Omid Salehi)

The newsroom – the beating heart of Bush
(Ian D. Richardson)

Voice: a monthly cultural programme renowned
for fighting fascism with word not sword
(BBC photograph)

The African Service with its largest audience rules the short waves
(Omid Salehi)

The Chinese Service broadcasts to the world's most populous country
(Bo Lutoslawski)

The Afghan Service, a 'sixth prayer' to its listeners
(Omid Salehi)

All the way down
(Orlando Gili)

Dash across the courtyard
(Orlando Gili)

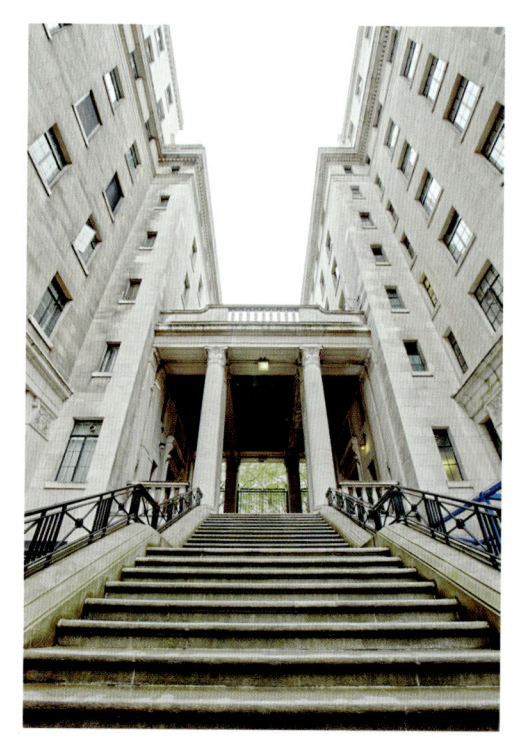

These stairs were the
first to see Alan Johnston's return
(Orlando Gili)

Cook Mohammad, who served food for thought as part of his menu
(Akbar Polat)

BBC Club, generally known as an unofficial newsroom
(Omid Salehi)

Keep your letters coming
(Nazes Afroz)

Hamid writing in residence
(Jennifer Chevalier)

Chapter Four

Rubbing Shoulders:
"Sorry, Where Did You Say You Were King of?"

Prince Charles c/o Bush House

For many people around the world Bush House was, perhaps, the only place in London they knew. We used to get letters from Africa that were addressed to Prince Charles c/o Bush House or the Queen c/o Bush House.

When I was running the Hausa Service we had a very splendid gentlemen coming to us from Hadejia, which is an emirate in the north of Nigeria, a trader who had to buy some hospital equipment. He came straight off the plane to Bush House, because he didn't know clearly where to go and the BBC Hausa Service was the best known address to him. So he was coming and asking my advice on where to buy hospital equipment.

Graham Mytton

Parting Shot

About a week after I joined the Bush newsroom in early 1995, we were visited by Prince Charles. After I'd exchanged pleasantries with him about my guide dog, my colleague Linda King, standing beside me, said to the parting prince that working at the World Service was rather like being at the United Nations. Turning to her, Prince Charles said: "Yes, but more influential."

Mark Pivac

The Royal Wee

In the early 1980s Princess Margaret came on a royal visit to Bush House. At some point one of our secretaries was deputed to take her to the ladies' lavatory, and was intrigued to see her turn on all the taps before disappearing into the cubicle to perform her ablutions. Plucking up her courage, she asked her on the way out why she had turned on all the taps. "Well, this is a broadcasting emporium, is it not?" she replied in her cut-glass accent. "And we wouldn't want anyone broadcasting the royal wee now, would we?"

Gordon House

"Sorry, Where Did You Say You Were King of?"

During the Second World War various heads of state were exiled in London and would come to Bush House to broadcast to Nazi-occupied Europe. I'm told one arrived late one evening and announced himself to the security guard at the entrance: "I'm the King of Norway and I've come to broadcast to my people." The security guard replied, "Righty-o" and phoned the studio: "I've got here..." Turning back to the visitor, he inquired, "Sorry, where did you say you were king of?"

David Prosser

Prime Minister Cut Short

On the 3rd of June 1990 Margaret Thatcher, the then Prime Minister, took part in a phone-in for the BBC World Service, answering questions from all over the world. I was allocated as the studio manager for this event. As you can imagine, we took it very seriously – I spent all morning checking every connection, phone line and microphone, and we had the full police presence and sniffer dogs routine before she came in.

Some years later the producer wrote in the *Guardian* about how "we in the cubicle" could see the realisation dawning on her that the whole world was listening to her every word: he concluded that the boost that this gave to her ego resulted in her leaving the World Service in peace at a time when she was attacking other parts of the BBC. I wouldn't know about that – and I had my hands full just keeping the programme running smoothly, so I hardly heard a word she said.

I should explain that World Service programmes run to a very tight schedule because of some transmitters joining and leaving as the peak listening hours move round the planet; transmissions start and finish to the second, and overrunning is impossible. I don't know whether anyone explained this to her – possibly not. Or possibly they did and she didn't listen.

The programme was supposed to finish at 45 seconds to 4pm; five seconds before this, Oliver Scott, the presenter, wrapped up neatly – and then the wretched woman tried to put in the last word ("and might I just say..." or something like that). This left me with three seconds to decide what to do, so I fell back on my training and the rule book and took her off air, mid-sentence, at the exact finish time.

Everyone in the cubicle looked a bit worried, and she looked thunderous just for a moment, but it passed over – and to be fair, no one ever suggested that I should have done something different.

I had to write a log, of course ("Prime Minister pot-cut to prevent an overrun" – a standard formula: "pot-cut" means "shut the fader rapidly"). Where it said, "What action should be taken to prevent this happening again?" I wrote, "General election." I didn't anticipate a palace revolution – and evidently neither did she.

So I may be the only person ever to silence Margaret Thatcher.

Roger Wilmut

"Was It You Who Booked a Phone Call to Margaret Thatcher?"

We thought very long and hard about what we can do to bring the Russian Service to a new level, and had this idea: why don't we invite the Prime Minister of Britain, who was at that time – just after the Perestroika started in July 1988 – very, very interested in the Soviet Union. This was unheard of: the first and probably the only time a phone-in with the British Prime Minister would be broadcast anywhere in the world outside this country. John Tusa wrote a letter, which was delivered in person to 10 Downing Street around 9:30 in the morning. The phone call from 10 Downing Street came in the afternoon: "When would you like Mrs Thatcher to do the phone-in?" We were gobsmacked.

At that time we had a new studio only just commissioned, never tested, never tried before, and I was allowed to do whatever I wanted. It was on the 11th of July 1988. She came, looked at the whole set-up and asked me, "Are you sure we will be able to stay on air for 59 minutes?" Being very sure of myself at that time I said, "Of course, Prime Minister," although there was no way for me or anyone else to know whether we would get any phone calls.

The studio was new, so we tested absolutely everything, apart from the telephone exchange at Covent Garden. Because it was swamped with phone calls from the Soviet Union, because we were tripping each other, out of 10 or 15 calls which were coming through the Covent Garden exchange, we were getting something like two or three in the studio. It was a minor disaster, but still we had more than 800 phone calls all in all.

She was fantastic in the studio. She would follow every instruction to a tee. It was great working with her but, as we were coming to the end of the broadcast, I told her, "Prime Minister, we are coming to an end" – and she looked me in total disbelief. She was prepared for two, three hours and it was only 59 minutes.

We finished the broadcast. I was trembling like a leaf. She came out of the studio, stormed into the cubicle and the first question she asked me was, "Why did you stop me?" I said, "Prime Minister, two hours ago you asked me whether we can stay on air for 59 minutes and now you are asking me, why didn't we continue?" Then she said something I'll remember for the rest of my life.

"I am only a Prime Minister, you are a professional, you should have thought" – and with that she smiled and brought two glasses of whisky and we drank together. I said, "Prime Minister, OK, next time we will do two hours, but you have to promise to bring Gorby to the studio," and she shook my hand: "Done deal".

The best feedback we had was from a cartoon in the *Daily Mail* depicting two burly gaolers somewhere in a salt mine in Siberia, handing a telephone to a tiny little dissident and asking him, "Was it you who booked a phone call to Margaret Thatcher?"

Yuri Goligorsky

Obviously a Political Guerilla

One African gentleman brought his bodyguards, who insisted on going into the studio with him rather than staying in the cubicle. I wonder whether they were armed.

On another occasion I was sent to a studio to record, I was informed, a Latin American guerilla. I went down expecting to find a large bearded man with dark glasses and a beret. In fact, he was a small, dapper gentleman with gold-rimmed glasses, a very expensive suit and an excellent command of English, who answered exactly the questions he wanted to answer and very neatly sidestepped the rest. Obviously a political guerrilla!

Roger Wilmut

Mr Psycho

We used to receive quite a lot of letters from Canada, we still do. It's just changed. The format is different now. There is this man who calls himself Psycho for some reason, Mr Psycho – that's his alias. He is known for posting a response to a debate, to a forum on our website, within a minute of its going live. I've tested it: we put up a discussion, on some emergency, for instance, or Benazir Bhutto's assassination – within a minute this man writes two paragraphs, very articulate. A lot of people are delighted to see their name on the BBC site. Sometimes they may not have interesting things to say but they just love the fact that their name is mentioned by the BBC. I actually met somebody who came to Bush House to visit the Urdu Service, and Shafi Sahib signed him in. As we were going around, he produced his visiting card, which read "BBC commentator", and I said, "But I don't know this man, we've never heard of him, we don't use him, how is he a BBC commentator?" It turns out, he is a regular contributor to forums on the Urdu website and the English website, so he calls himself a BBC commentator.

Waheed Mirza

It's All Hindi to Him

In 1949, or about that time, the Hindustani Service started producing dramas but the scripts were mostly translation of English plays. Once Aslam Malik produced his translated script of *Murder in the Cathedral* and was able to bring T. S. Eliot to Bush House to listen to it. Eliot sat in a studio but I really doubt if he was able to understand it.

Iqbal Bahadur Sarin

Indians I Have Met

The Hindustani Service had a series of programmes called How I Earn My Living. There were quite a few Indians living in London, doing small jobs, such as repairing shoes, selling samosas, putting up stalls at village fairs for fortune telling and working as pedlars. They used to earn 15 to 20 shillings a day, which was reasonable at the time. There was another programme called Indians I Have Met. I happened to meet a stable keeper, who was a smooth talkative person and helped me to make an interesting programme. Then we had a series called Today's Guest. For that I interviewed some personality and when, after his interview, I presented him with a modest cheque, he accepted it with the remark that he would get it framed as it was the first time that he had earned money for his own labour.

Iqbal Bahadur Sarin

Vaclav Havel in Casuals

The BBC exhibition in Prague in the early 1990s had closed for the day, and we thought we had an afternoon off. We were heading for a walk when a call came through that President Vaclav Havel had agreed to an interview with the head of the Czech Section, Terka Javorska. She wanted to dash straight round to the presidential palace but said we couldn't go dressed like this. I agreed. I was wearing an old polo shirt and she was wearing jeans.

We ran back to our rooms and met again as soon as we could, slightly flustered and breathless but now dressed for the occasion, she in a posh frock, me in a suit and tie. When we arrived at the palace, the president's aide was waiting for us. He took us past the sentries in newly-designed Czech uniforms, marching to a newly-choreographed, distinctively Czech step, across the historic courtyard and up a broad staircase.

Our guide knocked on the large oak door of President's office. "Come in!" called a voice inside. The aide led us in and presented us to Vaclav Havel, who stood up and held out his hand to greet us with a smile.

He was wearing a Rolling Stones T-shirt and jeans.

Hugh Closs

Shrewd Minister

In a scene almost exactly replicating one in Nigel Balchin's novel *The Small Back Room* (where a visiting minister, being shown advanced wartime technology, is only interested in an ordinary adding machine), we had a VIP visitor who sat in during a transmission of our hour-long live magazine programme Outlook. It was quite an exciting show, but at the end of it the only thing he chose to comment on was the fact that elapsed time counters on the two tape recorders which we'd been using had got out of sync by two seconds (which is normal enough, given manufacturing tolerances and slippage). He seemed to think he was making a rather shrewd observation. Worrying, really.

Roger Wilmut

World Success

The most famous broadcast of the French Service was, without a doubt, the speech given by General de Gaulle on the 18th of June 1940, calling on free Frenchmen to join him in London. However, no recording was made. The only one, played sometimes in documentaries, was made on the 22nd – not in Bush House since the French Service moved there only later.

However, another French Service recording, definitely made in Bush House in the early 1970s, was heard by millions, although most of those who heard it never knew what it was. Pierre Le Sève, who died in April 1979, had sent some tapes of his regular Flash Touristique programme to Paul McCartney's team, who were preparing the album *Band on the Run*. They used the material in the song "Picasso's Last Words". *Band on the Run* was a world success. But Pierre said later he had great difficulty in getting paid, and eventually received a fee of about five or six pounds.

Xavier Kreiss

Derek Walcott Well Disposed

A great thing about working for the BBC World Service was that you never had to beg for an interview with a writer, except occasionally. The last series that I produced was called Caribbean Voices – it looked back to the programme of the same name, the one which kick-started the careers of V. S. Naipaul and Derek Walcott. I was determined that Walcott would appear on the programme; I rang him up at his home in St Lucia and laid it on thick. He was Caribbean writing personified, I had read everything he had ever written, he'd explained my life to me! I was so indebted to him, I was his biggest fan, he was even more important to me than V. S. Naipaul. Walcott let me talk and talk until I finished my piece. There was silence at the other end. Eventually a growly voice came down the line: "What's the fee?"

Colin Grant

Mohammed, the Tea Boy

There was a time – in the late 1990s, I think – when Benazir Bhutto and her retinue visited Bush House. Among the numerous accompanying dignitaries was a very young man who appeared to be her tea boy. As the Prime Minister was making her way through the Centre Block to the South East wing, a call came through that she was required urgently to fly back home to deal with another crisis. But no sign of Mohammed the tea boy. A search was launched throughout Bush House with Bhutto announcing that she couldn't wait for him. He was eventually found in recruitment, inquiring about getting a job with the World Service. How's that for initiative? By that time the Prime Minister was, no doubt, well on her way back to Islamabad.

Alastair Lawson-Tancred

Exactly as It Was During the War

During the Second World War the Norwegian royal family had escaped the country and King Haakon and Crown Prince Olav did many broadcasts to the nation from Bush House. At some point in the 1980s, an anniversary programme was being made and the former Crown Prince, by then King Olav, was visiting Bush House. When he was shown into the studio he had broadcast from all those years ago, he enthusiastically exclaimed, "Oh, how lovely, you've restored everything to exactly as it was during the war!" – whereupon his minders had to admit, somewhat blushingly, that no, it just hadn't been upgraded in the intervening years.

Hild Myklebust

Without Prior Warning

Members of minor royalty from around the world coming to Bush House is nothing new. I am sure they were happy to come to see us and have the opportunity to meet the many creative types here. In the spring of 2007 we were expecting a visit from HRH The Duke of York. On such occasions extra security measures are taken, with security officials coming to all areas of the building the VIP is visiting in advance. This is done confidentially and without prior warning.

Quite early one morning I was in the office (a very quiet corridor on the third floor of the Centre Block, which goes nowhere) preparing some breakfast for myself, when a springer spaniel came hurtling into the office, at speed. It wasn't expecting to see me and I definitely wasn't expecting to see it, so I parted company with a whole bowl of cornflakes and a nearly full box of the same. The dog and I had a tussle until the handler arrived and I explained that I worked for the director, who the Duke was coming to visit, and that it wasn't my intention to try and poison their dog with some Crunchy Nut Cornflakes.

Karen Fotheringham

"*But There Is no Pilot*"

The scene is Baku Airport one summer day in the early 1990s. Assorted local people are walking, sitting or lying around – in the hope of boarding a plane. The schedule for departures is only an approximate guide to reality.

Out of a taxi into this airport scene stepped a group of four foreigners: Behrouz, Yuri, Peter and I. Our mission was to obtain local rebroadcasting facilities for the shortly to be launched services (in local languages and English) in the former Soviet Central Asian and Caucasian Republics.

Our team thought we had fared quite well in Baku, so it was with a spring in our step and with hopes of more progress at our next destination that we arrived for our flight. We were armed with real tickets for what we thought were real schedules, purchased in real money at prices which locals hanging around the airport could never have afforded, but which – as things eventually turned out – easily covered the fuel cost for a planeload of people heading, like us, for Chimkent.

Chimkent began to seem a suspiciously distant prospect when we discovered that our scheduled flight was not happening that day. The reason was that there was no plane available to take us. Yuri thought for a few moments, looked around and took command of the situation. "Andrew," he said, "you must look angry. I am going to tell these people that you are an extremely important person, not accustomed to being messed around; a failure to fly our party promptly to Chimkent could have the most serious consequences for the imminent state visit of President Aliyev to Great Britain – and for those officials involved at this end. But, Andrew, you must look angry, for when I speak with these officials I shall be directing their gaze towards you, pointing you out."

Yuri went through the routine of engaging with these officials, returning each time to where our group was waiting and reminding me of my essential duties. This reminder was necessary, since the wait, though long, was for me extremely interesting. I was particularly intrigued by a little old lady who had stacked up an improvised small log fire on which she was cooking, seemingly to sell, small pieces of what might once have been a chicken.

Returning to us after another reprise of his carefully constructed charade, Yuri announced: "There is a plane." Before we could get too excited, however, he added: "But there is no pilot, so, Andrew, you must still look angry!" With these words he marched back to the airport officials. A little later, his triumph was complete. A pilot had been found. It was necessary only to make ready the plane.

Readiness, as we discovered on boarding a more than averagely aged Tupolev, did not mean readiness Emirates or Cathay Pacific-style. Thankful for small mercies, we settled ourselves into the quaint and mildly tatty cabin: a living room with wings, wheels and small oval windows – and, we trusted, mechanically complete. Any expectations of an apology for the delay were dashed by the demeanour of the air stewardesses who walked through the cabin as if the passengers were an irritant to their personal flying experience. But what the hell? Three hours earlier we would have given anything to be on a plane, even this plane, rattling along the runway, headed for Chimkent – and knowing that the BBC's money had rescued a hundred and fifty or so other people who would still have been hanging around Baku airport.

Andrew Taussig

A Democratic Leader

There was an occasion when Robert Mugabe, then the leader of ZANU, living in Maputo and in Mozambique, came in to be interviewed by Focus on Africa, wearing a black leather jacket, and queued for lunch in the canteen like everyone else.

Mike Popham

Acronyms and Pedagogical Pop

I joined the BBC in 1972 and, after a couple of years as a studio manager, transferred to ExR&Tel (English by Radio and Television – the BBC in those days liked acronyms, and memos were unintelligible unless you could decrypt the identities of HFES, AHCT&F or HPOps). The department had been producing English language teaching programmes since July 1943. It had been transferred from Bush House to Queens House, at 28 Kingsway.

I joined at a time of rapid expansion. The radio programmes were taken by 250 stations in 100 countries. The major series were usually recorded with actors from the BBC English by Radio, which had its Green Room in the North East wing. The 100 yards which separated Queens House from Bush House enabled producers whose programmes were late and somewhat overlong to hide in an editing channel somewhere. It was possible to vanish for several days, by which time the missing tapes had been cut to length. The 100-yard gap also encouraged a sense of community: one Christmas pantomime included a guest appearance by Barbara Goldsmid as Fairy Godmother. (Plus one by a producer – I won't mention his name – who felt that fishnet tights were just his thing.)

What I remember most about Queens House is the constant and varied stream of visitors from around the world. There was no reception, and they just walked in along a rather baroque tiled corridor and took the lift up to the third floor. Soviet TV bought the BBC English by Television series Songs Alive and spent some time with us. A group of Chinese teachers arrived in near despair: they'd come to the end of a good visit to the UK and the English language schools they'd visited had donated books to them. The books had just been confiscated by Chinese Embassy officials as unsuitable on ideological grounds. Finally, one day a Hungarian teacher of English slipped quietly in and left a bottle of whisky, saying how much her pupils enjoyed Pedagogical Pop, a series of mine teaching the words of pop songs.

Hamish Norbrook

Man of the Year

The Hausa Service listeners voted Saddam Hussein the Man of the Year. Apparently the Foreign Office called to say, "Is this what we've been paying you for?" At that time, I thought I was going to be sacked. I was scared because I thought they were going to put me in prison.

Isa Abba Adamu

The Great and the Good

Working for the BBC in Bush House, it was easy to meet the great and the good. As a publicity officer for the BBC German Language Service, I notched up my fair share of German Chancellors and British royalty. But one encounter was particularly memorable. For the German Service's 50th anniversary in 1988 I had put together materials on the service's history, with contributions from its former staff. Renate Harpprecht-Lasker was among those who wrote about their time in Bush House. When the British liberated Belsen concentration camp in April 1945, Patrick Gordon Walker interviewed the young Renate and her sister Anita in the camp for the BBC. She recalled it was difficult to explain and describe what had happened to her and around her. As a result of this broadcast, the sisters found they had relatives in England, one thing led to another, and in the spring of 1946 Hugh Carleton Greene, the head of the German Service, took Renate on. She rose from a secretary to an announcer and a presenter, and her long love story with the German Service lasted until 1959. Those years in Bush when she was badly paid but happy were unforgettable, she wrote. I am looking at a letter from her right now. I met her in 1988. We had lunch together, and there were so many things I wanted to ask her that day but I skirted the issue, afraid to wake painful memories in her. I was young, of a generation born after the war, but still somehow feeling responsible for what had happened in my country in those dark years. I looked at this elegant woman sitting across the table from me; nothing betrayed what she had suffered. I felt strangely moved and curiously distant at the same time – it was as if fate allowed me a moment's glimpse of something that I would never fully comprehend.

Gunda Cannon

"He Probably Is the Sierra Leonean Prime Minister"

I can remember a certain Miss Taylor, a receptionist at Bush House. She rang me up to say, "There is someone here who claims to be the Sierra Leonian Prime Minister. Shall I tell him to go away?" "No, Miss. I think you should let him in. He probably is the Sierra Leonean Prime Minister."

Robin White

Stuck in a Lift

The BBC World Service started broadcasting for Central Asia and the Caucasus in the summer of 1994. A lot of effort went into securing FM re-broadcasting in Azerbaijan, and a state visit to Britain by President Heidar Aliyev looked as if it might be helpful in our negotiations on the ground.

The mood at the time, as Azerbaijan and the other former Soviet republics were establishing themselves as independent states, was friendly, positive and open – despite various problems. Azerbaijan had just fought and lost a war with Armenia over the enclave of Nagornyi Karabakh. The Azeris had a tendency to see Armenian foul play in any obstacle or setback.

President Aliyev was invited to Bush House where he was met by the chairman of the BBC governors, Marmaduke Hussey. I was there as the head of the Russian and Ukrainian Service.

The Chairman greeted the President in the car park and immediately impressed him. Duke Hussey was a big man. He walked with a stick, and painfully, after leaving one leg in Italy during the war. We moved towards the Centre Block lifts which the uniformed commissionaires had put specially into manual operation for the President's ride. Hussey, Aliyev and I got into a lift with half a dozen heavily built Azeri security men. The commissionaire shut the doors and the lift started to rise. It came to a halt between floors and there we stuck.

The commissionaire, deeply embarrassed, contacted all of the right people. House services did everything they could to rectify the situation. Hussey stayed enviably cool and treated everyone to British humour. But, as the delay went on, the security men became more agitated. Aliyev himself was becoming worried. Was it possible that they walked into an Armenian plot in Bush House? Still the lift refused to move. The security men's hands were beginning to move to the bulges under their jackets.

Eventually we were wound up to the third floor by hand – a more energetically manual operation than the commissionaires had envisaged. The doors were cranked open and we were released onto the marble landing. The bodyguards eased up and the mood began to lighten as the chairman led the President down the corridor past the black and white photos of former World Service directors.

Once in the director's office, Hussey broke the tension with an extraordinary gesture. He presented Aliyev with one of his favourite VIP gifts – a heavy BBC-branded paperweight. And, as he did so, he explained that this very solid gift could be used by the President, if the need arose, to crush his enemies. Aliyev, once the head of the KGB in Azerbaijan, warmed to this politically incorrect remark. Pleasant and productive discussions ensued.

For several years BBC Azeri was broadcast by the state radio of Azerbaijan on its national network.

David Morton

"Good Boy, He Will Go Far..."

After getting stuck in a lift and being presented with a paperweight ("to punish those who don't listen," said the then BBC chairman), Azerbaijani President Heydar Aliyev was interviewed in several languages (being fluent in Russian and Turkish as well as Azeri) for various BBC World Service programmes.

I have done two of those – in Azeri and in Russian – under the Azeri TV cameramen's watchful lenses recording the President's every step in London.

The interviews recorded, Mr Aliyev shook hands with those present in the studio. He held mine for a second and asked: "Have I seen you before, young man?" Before I could think of an answer, his English interpreter stepped forward and gave a short but frighteningly informative report about my birthplace (in Aliyev's Azerbaijan it is very important), my education and previous employment.

Well, the interpreter didn't know that Heydar Aliyev actually met me before, in 1979, when he was ruling Soviet Azerbaijan as a Communist Party leader and I was a schoolboy entrusted with making a speech on behalf of Azerbaijan's schoolchildren at a party conference.

When I finished the speech and walked along the presidium to get off the stage, I heard Mr Aliyev saying: "Good boy, he will go far..."

Famil Ismailov

At Least One Important Listener

We knew we were in for it. What a bleak city Kinshasa was. Mobutu and his cronies, before they fled, had stripped out everything of value. Our FM relay, recently installed, was at the top of a large shopping complex. When we had arrived at the foot of this monolith that morning, we were told that our equipment was on the 43rd floor, but that there was no lift.

There was no lift, there were no cables, there were no shops; everything had gone with Mobutu, had been looted thereafter. The whole thing was like a huge multistorey car park but with no cars – nothing but concrete. On the 43rd floor there was a metal door, opened at our knocking by two armed guards. Inside it was like something out of James Bond – spotless equipment, order and cleanliness throughout. Below lay the vast impoverished city with its wide slow river.

Then the call came to attend President Kabila, who had welcomed us into the country to install our own FM frequency and to form a partnership with the State Radio and Television which had been utterly pillaged by Mobutu's men. The President was not going to intervene in our recent deals, but our resident correspondent would have to leave the country as soon as possible. His attitude was wrong and the government could not answer for his safety.

There followed the most difficult and worrying of conversations: if a government said that it could not guarantee the safety of a reporter, you had to get them out, quickly. However, it seemed to us that the President's heart was really not in this threat. We went through our usual spiel: "Please give us every detail of anything you might think is inaccurate, and we will certainly investigate." But his attention seemed to wander. We said that if the person did have to leave, we would have to issue a press release to explain why. The President looked at his aides. His instincts were clearly for free speech. He called for tea.

As a lackey arrived with the tea, the President's personal computer was swung round. We all saw Arsenal Football Club on his screen saver. People smiled. Our man, Michel Lobelle, mentioned Kanu, an African footballer who at that time played for Arsenal.

Things improved. The popular part of the BBC's broadcasts on FM was not so much the BBC French Service, nor even the English stream as far as news was concerned – no, it was the Saturday afternoon sports programme. Yes, the Premiership had led us to many an FM deal, and it was the cement in Kinshasa, too. The talk turned to Kanu's recent hat-trick against Chelsea.

Then the President said: "Please tell your young man to be fair." We said that we would. "We have a very difficult situation here; we can be very easily criticised. We are trying our best. Opening the airwaves is part of this change. But please, be fair." It was impressive. It would be hard to find any country in the world more difficult to run. His own father had been murdered. Without compromising any of the BBC's principles, there was sympathy among us. It was not the usual rant: it was something much more noteworthy.

Our young man was not thrown out. When we spoke to him that evening we made clear that he should not change his principles. But we did repeat what the President had said. We reminded ourselves also to ask Alan Green, in his weekly football programme, to perhaps do another profile on Kanu. We knew he would have at least one important listener here in Kinshasa.

Barry Langridge

Canteen Antics

Security in Bush House was non-existent. There were two reception desks in those days. You could tell a receptionist who you wanted to see, or you could just walk in like the staff did. You could hang up your coat in the ground floor wardrobe and take a ticket, which doesn't happen any more. And the canteen, of course, was famously open to all. There was a rumour that someone once had the switchboard announce over the tannoy: "Could King's College students please finish their lunch and leave because the students of the London School of Economics are waiting."

Milada Haigh

Spies Galore

Bush House was rife with spies. Before the Berlin Wall fell, this building was known to be full of agents from eastern Europe. Even with people who came over from a tame communist country like Yugoslavia, there were attempts by secret services to recruit them. There was very little to spy on, but we always knew who was reporting on conversations in the office. We came to London knowing that it was fairly possible that somebody was spying – this had been a long-standing practice during the Cold War. It was inevitable that some of the people who joined the BBC had previously been recruited by somebody's secret service.

So, yes, the building was chock-a-block with spies. I once heard Bush House in the Cold War years described as a place with institutional green paint on the walls and various characters walking down corridors, smoking rank cigarettes and muttering to each other conspiratorially. The place was always fuggy, everybody smoked and there was a lot of conspiracy going on.

Maja Samolov

A Different Kind of Smoke

I once produced a Ghanaian group Dagarti in a Bush studio and noticed they were smoking while playing – nothing unusual about that in those days in the late 1970s, except for one thing. When I abandoned the talkback in the cubicle and went in to talk to them I discovered that they were smoking joints. I could only hope none of the bosses or BBC governors were about to make an informal tour of the studios.

Mike Popham

The Writhing of the High Commissioner

British Ambassadors and High Commissioners always had a mixed time with the BBC. In their pomp they were anxious that the BBC might say something unfortunate, even if it turned out to be true. The wiser and more experienced Foreign Office types kept a decent distance away from us, but would always help quietly if needed: if a BBC employee was in trouble, or if we were negotiating with the host government for broadcasting rights. But the nervy ones could be a nuisance. Early one morning in Bush House I had a blasting down the phone from a British official in Ivory Coast, telling me to apologise, on air and immediately, for two huge mistakes made by that morning's Network Africa. The programme had reported that students had been defenestrated by government troops in a northern town, and that tanks had been spotted on the street. "You will hasten this country towards civil war," was the Ambassador's warning.

I checked the recordings; I asked the editor to look into it immediately and then I rang the Ambassador to say that we and other broadcasters had several witnesses to the murder of the students, and that we had not reported "tanks"; we had reported armoured cars, and again it was accurate. As free speech was encouraged in Africa, attitudes to the BBC soon became softer.

At the opening of the new BBC's FM installation in Dar es Salaam the local High Commissioner appeared uneasy. The President was to be the star guest. Should the High Commissioner keep in the shadows, as this was a BBC function – or should he be seen close to the BBC, or close to His Excellency, who, unusually among African presidents, arrived on time, and seemed rather jovial?

The President shook the envoy's hand and then strode up to me and said: "Ah, you are the BBC boss; I have a question for you. It is a question that all Tanzanians want to ask – and we expect the BBC to tell us the truth." The High Commissioner stole closer, listening with great attention. What had the BBC done this time? Were the precious relationships between the countries about to be damaged? "You see," said the President, "in our country when we men are young we have to take a wife, often it is arranged for us. But when we grow rich or powerful we often leave the old wife to take a young and beautiful new one. Our question, Mr BBC, is this: why is the heir to the British throne doing the opposite?" The High Commissioner now started to wipe his hands like Uriah Heep on a bad day and pretended to look at his feet. "Your Prince of Wales is now getting old; he is not very handsome any more – yet he has had the good fortune to marry a young and beautiful lady." Indeed he had, we all agreed. The High Commissioner began to writhe. "So why has he taken as a mistress a plain old lady who wears Wellington boots?"

I laughed – but the High Commissioner almost writhed himself into the ground. He was torn between his duties: to protect the name of the Crown under all circumstances and, as is the case for all envoys, always to laugh at a presidential joke.

"So, Mr BBC, we all wait for an answer." "Sir," I said, "while it is true that the BBC knows many things, we cannot answer this crucial question." "Because it is beyond comprehension," said the President. "Your Diana is so lovely; we all adore her. And the old lady is so plain. Very, very strange. Now. You have brought equipment and training." "We have." "And do you know Robin White?" "I do." Again the High Commissioner's hands trembled and clasped each other. Robin White – that rude fellow who never had any respect… "And Bola Olafunwe; Elizabeth Ohene?" "I work with them all." "Please tell them we want to see them here. We want them to run the training." "I'll see what I can do." The President and his surprisingly modest retinue moved on.

"What happens now?" the High Commissioner whispered to me. "The Swahili service is going to interview him." The President sat down with Ali Saleh and Tido Mhando and submitted to the fixing of a mike and earphones. People waved for silence. The High Commissioner watched intently. This would be heard by around twenty million people in East and Central Africa. Would the President try the same sally about Prince Charles and his bedmates? The diplomat would never know: he was still taking elementary Swahili lessons every morning at breakfast on his lawn.

It was a worry for him. But I knew that the High Commissioner had to make a weekly report to London. He probably seldom had much of substance to include. This week, though, he had been a guest at a large function and had shaken hands with the President. I supposed that in this confidential weekly note he would not mention the presidential little joke.

Barry Langridge

"Well, That Was Great Fun, Wasn't It?"

One really good example of how the relationship between the BBC and the Foreign Office worked was at that time when there was much strong criticism from Saudi Arabia. David Gore-Booth, then Britain's Ambassador in the country, was getting it in the neck from the Saudis and kept saying to them, "Well, actually, I don't control the BBC."

So he invited me to go out to Riyadh. He gave a lunch party and invited, as he explained to me afterwards, the 12 people who were most critical of the BBC Arabic Service. They proceeded to hammer away at me over the lunch table, while David sat there with a benign smile on his face saying nothing. The party lasted over two and half hours. And when they all left at the end, he said, "Well, that was great fun, wasn't it?"

Sam Younger

"Who Are You?"

A newly trained Bush House studio manager was concentrating on his live broadcast one day, when he became aware that someone had slipped quietly into the cubicle behind him and was watching him. It went like this: "Who are you?" "Curran." "What do you want?" "Just having a look." "Where are you from?" At this point the intruder made a triangle with both thumbs and forefingers, saying "BBC?" while tapping its apex. It was, in fact, Charles Curran, the BBC director general.

Barry Mitchell

Books Talk for Themselves

"Have you read the book?" a writer would occasionally ask when, as a producer of a books programme, I was deputising for the presenter when conducting the interview. It was a question that didn't fill me with dread. Up until my last years in the Arts Unit, it was always a code of honour that you read the book – indeed, it was built into your working week, a day was assigned for reading.

When V. S. Naipaul came to Bush House in 2001 he first mistook me for a valet, it seemed, handing me his splendid fedora to hold for the duration of his time in the building. Once he had sat down and made himself comfortable, he turned to the presenter, Harriet Gilbert, and said rather drolly, "Now what do you want to talk about? Of course, I am not going to talk about writing. One has done the work, the books talk for themselves." It took all of Harriet's considerable charm and determination to remind Sir Vidiadhar that he was appearing on a program called Meridian Books and that it came with an expectation that books would be discussed. Books were always being discussed. Those were the days when producers were almost in love with what they were doing and certainly in love with literature.

Colin Grant

Black Power in Life and Fiction

While working on The Morning Show in the early 1970s, I was sitting at my desk one morning, minding my own business when a fierce-looking black man, who had a day or two earlier proclaimed himself to be God on air in an interview with our presenter Pete Myers, turned up. He was there, he said, to collect his contract – not much for a self-proclaimed deity – of £7.75 or some such derisory sum for his appearance. He was accompanied by an obviously stoned white woman. The man was a former Boston gangster known as Hakim Jamal, a cousin of Malcolm X, who had built up quite a reputation as a charismatic proponent of Black Power. His lover was Gale Benson, the daughter of Captain Leonard Plugge, a former Tory MP who had started Radio Normandy and had connections with Radio Luxembourg. While Jamal was insulting the editor of the programme by calling him a "honky", Gale asked me chillingly if I would like to see the plans for the mass extermination of black men in the United States. I thought the best tactic was to remain calm and replied: "Yes, of course." Looking amazed, she said: "*Time Out* didn't want to know."

Eventually, they left. A few weeks later, I turned on the radio to hear that Hakim Jamal and Gale Benson had been cutlassed and buried in Trinidad. V. S. Naipaul, a former member of the Caribbean Service, afterwards wrote a novel about the murder called *Guerrillas*. I told Naipaul about this after he had appeared on the World Book Club in the early 2000s.

Mike Popham

Look of Disapproval

I mainly did clerical work at Bush House, but I also made programmes and for the last six months I was a lexicographer working on the BBC dictionary. I remember vividly how much P.D. James disapproved of the dictionary. If you don't believe me, there are some photos where she is pictured with the BBC governor – the look on her face tells the whole story.

Anthony Rudolf

An Old Etonian

A studio manager on his first day in Bush House went into the engineers' room saying, "Hello, I'm Simon Fernie – anyone else here from Eton?" – which, as you can imagine, didn't go down terribly well. For many years in Bush he often wore his Old Etonian tie. Fortunately nobody seemed to know what it signified. Once, around the time of the 70th anniversary of the World Service, he invaded Mark Byford's office and gave him a talking to when retired members of staff were prevented from entering the building without an official "retired staff" pass. He also used to edit tape, rather ostentatiously, with scissors instead of a razor blade.

Mike Popham

Never Less Than Twelve in Number

Julia Massey was one of the titans of Regional Administration at Bush House, working at the centre of the Asia and Pacific offices. The bane of her life were delegations – especially the Chinese who always wanted to come to London in apparently earnest attempts to discuss closer relations with the BBC. But nothing ever came of their visits.

Julia's opinion was that there was never any real substance behind the Chinese blandishments. Bits and pieces of English by Radio were mooted, in large meetings (the delegates were never less than twelve in number), but somehow the visit would end without anything formally agreed. Long speeches of thanks were made, and then it was everybody off to karaoke in the West End, and a promise to return with a substantial deal, next time.

The new regional head could not understand why his predecessor had put up with all this, but actually the reason was simple. Although we were barred at every turn, our short-wave signals jammed, we simply had to hang in there and work, hoping that things might change. China was too large a market to give up on.

What really irritated the new head was that the delegations would thin and slip off during working hours. Julia, who had done all the organising, knew why. "They're all out shopping," she said bitterly. "Clarks shoes, Burberry bags, M&S, Liberty." I protested that all those shops were now present in China. "No, they want the stuff from London, in the original bags, with the original tags. That's what counts."

The head resolved that this could not go on and prepared to say so. But at the final meeting new ideas were dangled before him. Perhaps when the next delegation came there might be co-productions – on AIDS, pollution, many such non-political themes. It was a possibility.

The head swallowed hard and found himself later that evening in a karaoke club (all paid for by the Beeb), trying to remember the words to Jim Reeves' "He'll Have to Go" as the bouncing ball went up and down on the huge screen in front of him. A very long evening lay ahead. And probably, in a couple of months, he might have to perform something by Ray Charles. Would it be unsubtle to give the next delegation "Your Cheatin' Heart"?

Barry Langridge

MI5 Finds Knitting

I was at Bush House from 1954 until I married in 1957. My first job was as a trainee production secretary working for the Arabic Service which was then broadcasting eight hours a day – it was during the Suez crisis. My husband-to-be worked as a research electronic engineer for Marconi Radar. One Friday he met me in London in his old 1934 Wolsey Hornet and we parked on the corner of a road in Soho. After dinner we went back to where we thought we had parked the car and it was not there, so we walked walked to the Bow Street police station and reported the stolen car.

Eric was concerned because he had left his luggage in the car, which included papers he needed for a business meeting he was to fly to, held to make sure communications were up to date because of the Suez crisis. Hearing this and the fact that I worked for the Arabic Service of the BBC, the police interrogated me and asked if I had told any of the Arabs about the papers. I knew nothing about it until then, so I told them that all I was worried about was the two-ply scarf I was knitting and had left on the back seat. MI5 was then involved and Eric's boss at Marconi informed, so we spent an anxious weekend worried Eric would be charged with leaving secret papers in the car and be out of a job. Anyway, I saw Eric off next Monday. He had been equipped with more papers, but I remember the MI5 detectives, looking like some James Bond characters in their trilby hats, taking him aside and asking him more questions before he left. The next day I had a telephone call from the police saying, "We have found your knitting." Of course, I was delighted. As it turned out, all the thieves had taken were Eric's camera, electric razor, other things – the papers were intact.

I then moved to a permanent job in the English Service of London Calling Europe, working for Elizabeth St. Johnston, who produced feature programmes such as Frontiers of Knowledge. We had some very interesting speakers including Francis Crick, Prof Lovell of Jodrell Bank, Dr Bronowski. My boss used to say, "Ducky, could you go and choose some music for the programme," and I would spend a pleasant time in the Music Library. Then there was, "Ducky, would you take these gentlemen over to the BBC Club and get them some drinks." I met a lot of very interesting people, amongst them the late Charles Wheeler, who was a news reporter then. Later, one day I was knocked down on a zebra crossing outside Bush House. People carried me back to the reception and by chance, Charles Wheeler was there. He cradled me in his arms on a bench until the ambulance took me off to Charing Cross Hospital. Luckily, I was only badly bruised and off work for a couple of days. Charles rang frequently to see how I was and I could only just speak as I had bruises to my face as well. We became good friends and kept it touch.

Working in Bush House had another important effect on me. I had been very young when the Second World War broke out, my parents didn't want me to be evacuated and I stayed in London during the Blitz, walking to school with a gas mask and an air raid helmet. I knew children and adults who were killed during the bombings, so I really hated the Germans. However, working for London Calling Europe I met many in the German Service, amongst them Gerhardt Puritz, the son of the famous singer Elisabeth Schumann. Gerhardt told me that, although he never wanted to take part in the war, he had no choice but to serve his country, so he was glad to be taken to a prisoner-of-war camp after being shot in his plane over Scotland. Making friends with him and others made me realise that the Germans were mostly just the same as the English, and it was only Hitler and others of his ilk who were hateful. It changed my attitude completely.

Ann Gildersleve

Jackets and Ties

We were always required to work in a jacket and tie, while World Service announcers were suited and booted. You never knew who might turn up in your studio. One day for me it was the Prime Minister, James Callaghan. One of my favourite announcers was Peter King. He once told me that he had problems naming his new-born son, having to be careful of names like Ray or Wayne. So he was called Toby. Fine, until some one observed: "The man born to be King!"

Barry Mitchell

A Good Stringer Is Gold Dust

Language services have for years relied on stringers, or local reporters. They are often at much more danger of threats or actual harm than staff reporters who are either visiting or on some short-term contract. A good stringer is gold dust. Wise news reporters cosset them, honour and respect them. Arrogant visiting reporters use their contacts and background wisdom but do not have the graciousness to refer to their help in despatches. Sometimes, in very tough places, the stringers themselves will ask not to be named – the risks are too high. When the shit hits the fan, the visitor will be safely on the plane or back at Bush House, while the local stringer has to duck and dive.

In Algiers, some years ago in the extremely violent days of a civil war, our information came from one source, who filed only in copy, which meant that his scripts were sent surreptitiously, to be read back at Bush House by producers, and he was never named. When I went out to meet him and offer him a months' break away on a trip, I found him through a complex network of contacts; it was like something out of Graham Greene. The final contact led me to a plain-looking shop. Through two internal doors I found our man. He was large, unassuming and impressive.

He and his wife were funded, in cash, to come to London and stay. He debriefed the Arabic, French and News Services. They took in a few sights. Then he went quietly back.

Barry Langridge

The Thursday Club

The BBC Club was a melting pot of journalists from many countries, and that collegiality helped to build up a rapport between different sections. During my time at the Bengali Service I never had any problem with Urdu-speaking people – we were all friendly despite our different opinions, particularly on the Bangladesh issue. Many Pakistani and Indian politicians also visited the BBC Club. My Bengali and Hindi colleagues and I used to entertain Jyoti Basu there, the then Chief Minister of West Bengal. I would like to pay tribute to the late Purshottam Lal Pahwa, who did a great deal towards this camaraderie. He founded what was called the Thursday Club, which was a gambling den where all shades and opinions gathered together, professors like Viqar Ahmad and iconoclasts like Yavar Abbas – anybody you could think of was a member of the Thursday Club and they sometimes used to go on all night. That really puzzled me when I joined the BBC, because Bush House doors were always open except when the Thursday Club was on. Then they went and sat behind closed doors, you never knew what was going on.

Shafik Rehman

Only Two Sycophants

We were in Abuja to get the blessings of the Nigerian Vice-President for our new FM partnership with Radio Nigeria. As we drove to his offices we received a phone call telling us to pull to the side of the road and wait. The President was leaving the country and the Vice-President had to go to the airport too, to see him off. All traffic stopped as a huge cavalcade rushed towards the airport, lights flashing and klaxons blaring.

Our new director of the World Service, who had never been to Africa before, had the following dialogue with our local partner and fixer.

Director to Partner: "I counted 15 vehicles for the President and 11 for the Vice-President."
Partner: "Correct. Two army cars at each end. Two dummy cars. The real car. A doctor's car, an assistant doctor's car and two media cars."
Director: "That leaves four cars. Who are they for?"

Partner: "Sycophants."
Director: "I see."
Partner: "The Vice-President is allowed two vehicles for his own sycophants. Two only."
Director: "I shall make a note of that for my own arrangements."

Barry Langridge

All Roads Lead to Bush

At a morning news meeting it was announced that Yul Brynner had died. One of the present, a bearded, scholarly man, an Englishman from the Russian Service, said meekly, "He was once my brother-in-law." It made me realise that most events in the world often had a tenuous connection with somebody in Bush House.

Mike Popham

A Motley Crew of Characters

Bush House was amazing. One could share a lift with the leading expert on China. I remember once in the canteen talking to someone who had been a Red Guard during the Cultural Revolution in China in the 1960s. I also recall that on the seventh floor of the South East wing there was a former German officer who had fought in the Battle of Stalingrad. And two floors lower down in the Russian Service there was a woman who had also fought in it, on the Soviet side.

One did learn a lot about contemporary history. Many of my staff were survivors of the Holocaust, many had been under German occupation during the Second World War. One very close friend was in Croatia when the Germans invaded and found that the Gestapo chief had been living in his flat. There were great many different characters in the English World Service and, of course, we thrived on outside contributors. I remember being the only member of the BBC staff in a studio, all the rest were MPs or experts of one kind or another.

David Wedgwood Benn

Chapter Five

Tower of Babel: "A Mini-Version of the British Empire"

A Babble of Many Voices

We don't want our memories to feel like a eulogy or a valediction – we want to go beyond and look how we can reform after 2012. The spirit and ethos of Bush House will definitely change but as a source of inspiration, I hope, it will remain.

When I went to the canteen for the first time, every table was a different continent, every language service was there, it was like Babel, benign Babel, a babble of many voices. Some people say Bush House is a mini-United Nations, but actually it's the opposite of the United Nations, which has always seemed to me extremely rigid, kind of bureaucratic and circumscribed, whereas Bush House at its best was really amorphous, energetic and vibrant.

Anna Horsbrugh-Porter

Retired Mujahid Solves the Biggest Technical Problem

When we were launching the Urdu website, the first thing that our new staff had to do was to learn to type in Urdu, which was a big step forward because none of them knew how to do that. By the time we got to that stage, when we started meeting up with the people who were developing this website, nobody investigated whether it was technically possible or not. Suddenly we realised that, actually, there was no Urdu dynamic font available which would allow us to run a 24/7 website. So we were stuck for a few months, looking around, writing to all these researchers, Microsoft and others, and everything seemed three or four years away. Everybody would say, "Yes, somebody's working on it, but it's not in any detailed form yet, it's not ready." And then somebody discovered a guy, a retired Afghan mujahid, who used to run this little software company in Peshawar. He said, "I have the solution." So we invited him over to Bush House, he hung around for a few weeks and sorted out the biggest technical problem that the World Service at that time was facing.

Mohammed Hanif

Urdu Online

I come from Kashmir and my first experience of the BBC Urdu Service was when I was growing up in the 1990s. It was compulsory listening in our household. Back then I did not think I would ever work for the BBC because my spoken Urdu was a bit rough and I had this rather proud provincial accent. I would never have got a job as a broadcaster, but when they started this online service around 2001 they recruited people like me.

In those days it was just a small web page, with short paragraphs in English and audio inserts which we physically copied from tapes and digitised. It was a laborious process but those were the beginnings. Little did we know that very soon there would be a party on the South Asia floor, celebrating 100,000 page impressions of the website.

When I joined there was no Urdu font available for the Internet. Most newspapers made images of Urdu text and uploaded them online, which the BBC thought wasn't the best way to run a website; you had to have editable text that you could update. Eventually they came up with a solution, which I thought was quite groundbreaking, although the font did not look good at first. British programmers found it incredibly hard to render a website in Urdu while writing programming code in English, left to right. I remember working with a developer on the seventh floor, late into the night, and she broke down. She cried because she just could not get Urdu text run from right to left in her code. To cut a long story short, it happened.

Waheed Mirza

Casting off the Shackles of the Raj

There was a time we were not authorised to edit any news items or even change the news order. Fortunately for us, we had in the Eastern Service, by design or by accident, a bunch of news writers who seemed to have cast off the shackles of the Raj and wrote objectively about current events. I will not name any names, but they were refreshingly unbiased writers. I can recall only one occasion when I refused to broadcast a talk that I considered heavily biased. The talk had originated – yes, you guessed it – from the newsroom, and I said as politely as I could in the Queen's English to my programme organiser that though I was prepared to translate the talk, I was not prepared to lend my voice to it. To his credit, he did not force the issue. To his greater credit, the talk was not broadcast by the Urdu Service.

Yavar Abbas

Translation Factory

The BBC was sometimes referred to as a translation factory. My personal challenge was that our translations had to be correct and emotion-free. At the Bengali Section we tried to do that, ignoring the repercussions at home because the BBC was branded "Bangladeshi Broadcasting Corporation". A lot of people would not meet me when they knew I was working for the BBC. The BBC had a problem of maintaining neutrality: on the one side, you had the Himalaya situation and Bengali aspirations, on the other there was the Pakistani government's standpoint. We as Bengalis felt that the BBC should not be neutral, that it should be on the side of Bengali independence, that was the feeling, but in our work that was certainly never reflected. Bengalis in the UK were another problem we had because they felt that my association with the BBC affected their relations' exit from Pakistan.

My listeners were Bengalis in East Pakistan. My first-hand knowledge and connections helped me to generate faith amongst the audience that the country would be independent some day. I'd like to mention three persons, Mr David Stride, Abed Hussein and Shyamal Lodh, whose input in 1971 was great.

Shafik Rehman

Bengali Diaspora Win Popularity for the BBC

Before joining the BBC in 1972 I was an outside contributor when still a student at LSE. We used to get two pounds and 10 shillings a week, which was good money then. When young and enthusiastic reporters from different parts of Bengal came together they had the energy and ability to create an atmosphere of a unified Bengali language pattern. This Bengali diaspora helped to win popularity and respect amongst listeners in both India and Bangladesh. A passionate debate over an appropriate word was quite frequent, which helped to reshape broadcasting at our section. We used to have discussions about a particular word, how to use it, how to be neutral and how not to avoid bias. Yes, we were translators but at the same time, we had a certain amount of freedom to decide what phrasing would be more appropriate.

Dipankar Ghosh

BBC Calls Bakwas

The BBC takes care that its credibility and impartiality remain intact. During the Bangladesh struggle for independence, the Defence Minister of India Jagjivan Ram said in a statement, "No, the other side is talking nonsense." I had to translate it. One difficulty was that our programme had to make it acceptable to the three warring countries, India, Pakistan and Bangladesh. We were all immigrants, we were treated as immigrants, but within ourselves we had to be careful. So when I was doing the news I mentioned the word for Jagjivan Ram's "nonsense", and my Pakistani friends were terribly upset, they felt that it was something that I had done deliberately, and it became so serious that they even threatened to burn Broadcasting House. Even my little daughter would ask her mother, "Are they going to kill my daddy?" Finally the BBC called Dr Ralph Russell, the vice chancellor of the School of Oriental and African Studies, and asked him to give his verdict on whether I had used the correct word to translate Jagjivan Ram's "nonsense". They called scholars to find out how "nonsense" can be rendered in Hindi and Urdu. The word was "bakwas" – it became a very big story. There was a headline in one of Pakistan's papers, the *Daily Jang*, "BBC Calls Bakwas."

I will never forget how much trouble that use of one word caused in the country. There was hardly any campus where they did not hold meetings threatening to burn BBC buildings. Once I encountered Charles Curran, the then director general, who had read about this in papers, and he asked me, "Mahendra, what are your plans for such and such day?" "I'll be in the office." "If I were you, I'd take the day off."

However much pain the BBC went to, I was the guilty party. A big meeting was called. Kenneth Lamb, the BBC public relations director in those days, came to it to represent the management. I said that I had no ulterior motive, I just found that was the only word and I used it – I would be the last person to do anything to hurt my own people. Then Kenneth Lamb got up and said, "What Mahendra did on his own initiative was to issue a statement and that was fair and he did the right thing. We have already collected all this evidence that 'bakwas' was used correctly. Ladies and gentlemen, I am here to confirm that the BBC has full faith in Mahendra Kaul's judgement." Then he suddenly got up and left the room.

Mahendra Kaul

The Rolls-Royce of Language Services

When a new programme organiser met the Urdu Service, which he now had to run, he was told by them that they were the Rolls-Royce of language services, that their journalism was peerless, and that, of course, Urdu was possibly the most fragrantly beautiful of all the world's tongues. It was a language close to that of Persian courts and Persian armies. All the other languages in the subcontinent of South Asia were ramshackle things.

The new Urdu head, in the rather colonialist style of Bush House in those days, knew very little Urdu and made the mistake of saying that many of its words did sound a little like Hindi, of which he knew more. There were looks of intense distaste. Hindi, it turned out, was a mere bastardisation of the pure and chaste Urdu – it was only there to let the Indians think that they had a real language of their own, which they did not: they wrote in a different way, but they all knew that Urdu was the pearl and the base of Hindi. As for Bengali and the Dravidian tongues of Southern India, they were barely worth mentioning.

"Hindi? Tell us, sir, can you name any Hindi poets?" Compared with Urdu and Persian poets, that was not to be thought of. All these Urdu journalists seemed to be poets; several wore cravats and two smoked pipes. When you went to their parties there were recitations. All very well, but the new boss decided to check on their claims in terms of journalism. Without telling them, he chose all the original scripts of a particularly heavy day of crises in the Middle East and Kashmir – and there was a complex item about Chinese pollution, too.

In those days, a language producer worth his salt would gather all the central materials on a subject. Mr Viqar Ahmad was particularly renowned for sitting in silence, looking at correspondents' reports, backgrounders, colour pieces and so on, all in English, and melding all these into a summary despatch for his audience. And then, on air, he would read this dispatch in Urdu, in a mellifluous tone.

The programme organiser secretly assembled a small group of journalists and professors outside the BBC, and furnished them with all the English original materials and with a back translation of Mr Ahmed's work into English (without, of course, naming him), plus a sound copy of the programme itself. The panel were all bilingual.

They then assembled, again in secret, to share their findings. The head had brought along a senior person from the English Scripts department – someone deeply suspicious of all our vernacular output. This would be the acid test, but there was little suspense because a man from SOAS immediately said: "Ah, this is Viqar, what a liquid voice he has." Another agreed. "But," said the head and the scripts person together, "tell us, what about the journalism of the finished piece? Is it fair, is it balanced, is it clear? Never mind the liquid voice; does it reflect the facts and the journalism of the English originals?" "The English original material?" said the SOAS gentleman. "Well, not quite."

"Aha", the central scripts person picked up his pen: "Can you tell us, then, in what ways Mr Ahmed's work deviates from those originals?" "Well, of course, it is far far better," said the SOAS man, and pushed the original materials away from him with a dismissive gesture. He seemed about to reach for a pipe. All the others nodded sagely.

Barry Langridge

Collegial Cordiality

I vividly remember that our language sections were not just translation factories churning out material issued by the centre. The Bush House newsroom, of course, produced news bulletins, while talks and features were prepared and discussed separately for each region. The advantage for us was that each Hindi and Urdu broadcast was heard and followed by the same listeners all over, in both languages, which is not at all difficult for either. And then there were some who would listen not only to Hindi and Urdu broadcasts, but also to Bengali translations. We as broadcasters could not afford to take sides; the common listenership ensured it.

What was the atmosphere like on our floor when the three language sections coexisted? I don't remember any occasion when these professional broadcasters from opposite sections argued with each other. The only single unpleasant incident was when some members of the Arabic Service made some passing remarks in a lift, venting their frustration with the events they were covering in the news. Our programme organiser trusted me to present a weekly London Letter, in which I replied to a listener's question about the relationship between different sections. I quoted a news story of a robber hijacking a car and taking its passenger hostage for 36 hours. In the end, when the passenger was rescued alive and the robber apprehended, a psychoanalyst explained that having travelled together for so many hours, the robber would not have found it easy to harm the fellow human being. Citing this, I asked how anyone could doubt our cordiality. We were working at the same place, doing the same job, under the same pressures and after finishing our transmissions, we went to have tea together in Bush House's famous canteen.

Kailash Budhwar

Language Services Viewed Affectionately

There were several language services in Bush House which were viewed affectionately – and with pride – by everyone in the World Service. The Nepali Service for its huge impact, despite its small staff, especially for its extended transmissions after the slaughter of the royal family. The Pashto Service with its gutsy reporters and wide reach. The Russian Service for having to face daily intimidation in Russia.

The Indonesian Service, which lost their stringer and many family members in the tsunami. In their day, when they still existed in Bush House, the smaller eastern European services were also admired.

You could pick your own list, but all lists would include the Burmese Service. Few staff, unassuming offices, serene charm, tea and fragrant flowers to greet you whenever you visited – but also a group with constant worries about the possibilities of closures or the continual demand for every service, no matter how tiny, to take "efficiency savings", otherwise known as cuts, of three percent each year. Small services were being bled dry, but they continued to deliver the goods.

Much worse for the Burmese Service were the profound personal problems of people who could never return to Burma, whose family members back there were always subject to bullying and harassment and whose contacts, anonymous, careful, but so brave, suffered for the cause. One regular, who had covertly supplied accurate information out of Rangoon for years, was arrested and sentenced to 14 years in jail – just for telling the truth.

The scepticism of Bush journalists was such that BBC-wide awards ceremonies were always greeted with indifference. Even when Hugh Saxby set up a World Service awards system, the reaction was: "And how much does this cost?" and "News will win everything because they've got all the money."

There was an external judging panel. Michael Palin was a speaking guest. Various categories were covered, to muted applause. The top prize went to the Burmese, and Palin could barely get the words out. Everyone jumped up, applauded, and many wept as Tin Thar Swe went modestly up to collect the award.

Barry Langridge

"All Hope Abandon, Ye Who Enter in"

Monday the 31st of December 1973. Strolling through revellers in Trafalgar Square, then down towards Bush House at the start of a night shift – one which brought out the wide range of cultures in Bush. Many listeners would have found the term "night shift" misleading. The programmes they heard were either in the evening if they lived in the South America or in the morning if they lived in the Far East. Hence terms such as "Hindi dawn TX". That transmission had one of the most delightful signature tunes, a flute melody that meandered along like the Ganges. (A pretentious simile that would have been scored through by any half-awake subeditor.)

The atmosphere was calm in most night-shift studios; dimmed lights, tired eyes peering at a script and checking the quality of sound. There were various technical requirements dictated by short-wave transmissions, robust, but not conducive to artistic excess. Try and run music under speech and a mishmash of both would result. But short wave reached its destination, at least in the judgement of the USSR. In 1989 I visited Tallinn, arranging radio and TV projects and lecturing. "Come and see the three sisters," came an ironic invitation one day. It sounded vaguely Chekhovian, but the sisters turned out to be three Soviet transmitting masts that had been used to jam western broadcasts.

A dodgy simile and a rank digression – typical of one's mind halfway through a night shift. Still another couple of hours before I could reasonably pop down to the canteen for some breakfast. Or, before it moved in November 1974, go outside for a walk round the old Covent Garden market. The premises were later turned into wine bars, but at the time you could wander around and hear merry Cockney repartee as a porter running along with a sack of carrots tripped over you.

That Hogmanay I was hoping for a Latin American carnival atmosphere, and fiesta time it was with Robinson Retamales and his crew – everything short of the samba down the corridor. I left them with a cheery "Feliz Año Nuevo" and went off to a succession of Far East transmissions. Chinese: "Happy New Year!" – "Sorry, not yet." Burmese: "Happy New Year!" – "Sorry, not till April." Thai: the same.

If many parts of a night shift could be soporific, anything involving newsroom would wake you up. For a studio manager a newsroom shift included recording incoming despatches from foreign correspondents and taking a selection along to studio S33 for Radio Newsreel. A plaintive inscription from Dante had been carved over the door: "Lasciate ogne speranza, voi ch' entrate" – "All hope abandon, ye who enter in." The writer had obviously encountered the newsroom practice of sitting on a despatch till the last possible moment, then charging through the door and handing it to a colleague with a cheery "Hope you can fit that in – it's a bit long and I'm not sure if it's been edited – and there were two or three false starts."

Hamish Norbrook

"I Didn't Understand a Word"

When the first Gulf War broke out, the regional management decided that they wanted to find out what we were saying. The manager did not want to rely on anyone in the Sinhala Service. They brought in a senior broadcaster from the Bengali Service to sit in on our broadcast. During the programme, he gave a running commentary to the manager about the contents of the programme. Watching this, we were intrigued as we knew that he did not understand Sinhala. Afterwards we asked him about what he was explaining to the manager. He replied, "I didn't understand a word of what you said, but as the manager wanted me to listen to your programme, I did so, and gave him a translation of what I thought you should say." We all had a good laugh about it.

Priyath Liyanage

Competition Within

Stringers had their own pride and their own loyalty. Sometimes the idea of "one BBC" did not percolate through to them very well. Often this was because, back in Bush House, the Arabic Service, for example, wanted to break the news first, and not share the goods with the French Service or anyone else, even though those might have an earlier bulletin.

Thus in Angola, the Portuguese Service stringer simply would not meet or talk to a youngster from Bush trying to report in English for Focus on Africa. The BBC Arabic man in Khartoum thought that the English-speaking correspondent from what is now Southern Sudan was a lesser being, not to be trusted. They seldom met. The two European female reporters in Nairobi, both British, but one with a loyalty to Focus on Africa, the other to BBC News, could never be persuaded to talk to each other, and certainly not to compare notes. You never saw both of them at a morning news meeting at our new Nairobi bureau. The Swahilis and the Somalis came to those meetings, but those two women never attended together, until one was, in effect, sacked.

Barry Langridge

Hamlet in Tamil

Some years ago I had acted as a studio manager on several episodes of *Hamlet* in Tamil. The Tamil producer was a splendid gentleman, cheerful, enthusiastic, committed to his work and unfailingly polite. I didn't work on the episode with the fencing match: apparently his enthusiasm led him to insist on participating in the duel himself, using one of the foils from the sound effects collection – he was waving it around like Errol Flynn. I have to say I wouldn't have allowed this – he had seriously impaired vision, and might easily have put someone's eye out; plus you don't fence with these swords, you point them downwards and bang them together or on a metal music stand.

For some reason in *Hamlet* Shakespeare identifies his gravediggers as Clowns. A literal interpretation of this led the producer to get the actors to perform in a very exaggerated comic manner, which apparently is the norm for comic characters in Indian drama but sounded rather out of place here. Most of it was convincingly done, however.

When we recorded the speech "O, what a rogue and peasant slave am I!" I commented to the English producer handling the technical side that it seemed rather short. She said, "Yes, he's cut it." I wondered if he cut "To be or not to be". "No, he liked that one so much he expanded it."

Roger Wilmut

A Driven Lot

I took over the drama slot from my predecessor when the bottle took him over. These were full-length plays, which we did in half-hour episodes every week. We had 45 minutes of transmission time, with 15 minutes of news and comment following weekly plays or other features. We did it on a fraction of the budget allocated for similar things today. We were a driven lot, and I remember agonising for hours and spending sleepless nights checking and re-checking Shakespeare lines, such as Othello's soliloquy before he smothers the life out of Desdemona. "Put out the light, and then put out the light." Or when the Bard really lays it on the line, throwing inhibition out of the window. This is Iago shouting to Brabantio: "'Zounds, sir, you're robb'd; for shame". And then: "You'll have your daughter covered with a Barbary horse; you'll have your nephews neigh to you; you'll have coursers for cousins, and gennets for germans." Whew, I had to translate that.

Yavar Abbas

Purifying Urdu and Modifying Hindi

It is rightly said that to be a good broadcaster you must be at home in the language in which you are broadcasting. The BBC Urdu Service was always very particular about it right from day one. You can't imagine the embarrassment I had to go through because of this tradition. My pronunciation and even spelling had always been quite bad. In my childhood Molvi Sahib used to teach me the Quran, and every time I made a mistake he told me that on the Day of Judgment God will punish me for my every wrong pronunciation. I am grateful to my senior colleagues at the BBC, who have over the years corrected me and, although it was very embarrassing at the time, I have a feeling that if God decides to conduct the proceedings on the Day of Judgment in Urdu, this training will save me quite a few lashes which I would have definitely received otherwise.

I remember a play produced by Yavar Abbas, in which a Pakistani and an Indian delegation meet in London to discuss some bilateral issues, but the language they are talking in is so "sanskritised" and "persianised" that an Urdu-speaking Englishman has to sit between them as a coordinator, with the purpose of translating their speech into simple Urdu, so as to make them understand each other. Although a satire, it was true. Immediately after independence, the tendency was to purify Urdu in Pakistan with unnecessary Arabic and Persian words, while in India they modified Hindi by replacing simple words with obsolete words of Sanskrit. Intellectuals in both countries resented these campaigns. However, the BBC continued to maintain its language according to the standards it had built over the years and that, in my opinion, was one of the reasons that kept it closer to its audience.

Ali Ahmed Khan

Moment of Aberration

One of the Olympian figures at the BBC was that of Anatol Goldberg, who was for many years a principle commentator with a somewhat mythical reputation. Scrupulously balanced and dispassionate, in the 1950s he was the subject of controversy as the head of the Russian Service, because apparently someone has told the Foreign Office, which funded the BBC Overseas Services, that the Russian Service was too appeasing in its tone.

He was a great man, a brilliant commentator, who not only spoke fluently and very wisely in English, but at the drop of a hat could switch to Russian, French, German or other languages, all with the same ease. It became known that he'd also acquired some knowledge of Chinese. One of the many stories about Anatol Goldberg, who had a very dry sense of humour, was the occasion when he was first hired by the BBC and the person interviewing him asked, "Mr. Goldberg, you speak Chinese. When did you learn Chinese?" Anatol is alleged to have responded, "In a moment of aberration."

Donald Armour

Eid at Bush

Back in the 1980s I was one of a group of Arabic specialist studio managers. We used to spend a week in one of the self-operated studios, 416 Centre Block: no windows, most often no one to talk to, especially during live recordings. That particular week it was approaching the end of Ramadan. I had been making efforts to keep a low profile while having any food as I felt it was cruel to been seen eating by any of the Arabic staff during their fasting. One day Dr Mahmoud Hussein, a lovely Egyptian fellow, very cultured, stuck his head round the door of 416 and said, "David, could you come to my office at about three o'clock this afternoon? We are celebrating the festival of Eid that is the end of Ramadan." Three o'clock came. I finished what I was doing and wandered along in the direction of Dr Hussein's office. It seemed that half of the Arabic Service were there, seated round quite quietly. He welcomed me: "David, have a whisky." My first thought was, "But you are not meant to... at any time." My second thought was, "But it is rude to refuse a genuine offer of hospitality from an Arab." My third thought was, "As they had been fasting for many hours, they might have had bad cases of indigestion, so it may be medicinal. In which case, permissible."

David Carlsen

Complimenting (the Wrong Kind of) Hair

There was no place at the BBC like Bush House. Lunchtime in the canteen sounded like Babylon. Numerous languages and cultures brought together created a mix that gave the World Service its unique atmosphere – and many memorable comic moments.

When a young Azeri team moved into rooms close to the Turkish Service, it was a great chance to get closer with our ethnic kin, and Azeri producers were very welcome to chat with their neighbours before the onset of programme deadlines.

One of the Azeris expressed his admiration to a veteran Turkish colleague, a lady who was cutting tape with an incredible speed, with the words, "I would love to be able to work like you." He didn't realise that in Turkish it sounded like "I would love to be able to caress you." The lady wasn't amused at all. To my colleague's luck, this exchange was heard by the then head of Turkish Service, Zeki Okar, an excellent linguist who had a long-standing interest in Azerbaijan. He jumped out of his cubicle and saved the day, explaining to the angry lady what was actually meant.

Azeris themselves were on the receiving end of language hiccups, too. Once, a senior editor, who spoke an Iranian version of Azerbaijani, wanted to compliment one of the Azeri female producers on her new hairdo – only he mixed up his words, referring to the wrong kind of hair altogether.

Famil Ismailov

"Just Like Tehran: a Corner Shop With an Azeri Sitting in It"

In Iran almost everyone speaks and reads the official language, Persian. But at home and in the street many Iranians speak other languages. Among them are Kurds, Arabs, Turcomans but the most numerous are Azeris, who make up almost a quarter of the population and who are very successful in Iranian national life. They have done well as soldiers, administrators and businessmen and in Tehran they are famous for their corner shops, their prominent vantage point allowing them to monitor the street and attract customers from all sides.

When the World Service started broadcasting in Azeri in 1994, the team was part of the Central Asia and Caucasus Service. It was headed by Behrouz Afagh-Tabrizi, an Iranian whose Azeri origins were clearly indicated by his surname, Tabriz being Iran's biggest Azeri city. Behrouz was given a corner office with windows looking in two directions, south towards King's College and west along the Strand, towards Trafalgar Square.

A few weeks after he moved in, Behrouz received a visit from Mozaffar Shafeie, formerly of the Persian Service, a Kurd, an actor with a huge talent for mimicry and an eye for the odd and the funny. He took one look at Behrouz's office and said: "Just like Tehran: a corner shop with an Azeri sitting in it."

David Morton

Just a Bloody Minute

Controllers of Radio 4 tremble when they have the impudence to change anything in their schedules. Radio audiences like to own the output they like. The World Service listeners are, of course, much more numerous and far more possessive.

So it was with nervousness that we launched a new English Service schedule for the Indian subcontinent. We had re-jigged the news timings, especially of our flagship Newshour, and moved From Our Own Correspondent and other news-related heavyweights. In a large hall in Chennai we watched as the place filled for our "Meet the BBC" question and answer session.

After a short introduction we said that we would now like to hear from the audience. No one stirred. A very old gentleman was helped to stand up. He leant on a stick. His acolyte also stood up and announced that this gentleman was the chairman of the BBC Listeners' Club, as well as a professor of English. He would ask the first four questions. We wondered whether this was fair or not, but then decided we could not intercede.

"My first question," said the old man, 'is this. Where is Mr Mark Tully? And if he is not among those here present, why is he not present? Does he not understand that here in this city is the very centre and hub of English literature appreciation in the country of which he is supposed to be an expert?"

We mumbled, but the professor was off and running. He was, among many other things, the originator and chairman of the Chennai George Bernard Shaw Society, yet he had never heard anything by Shaw on the BBC. He was also the chairman of the Chennai Tamil Association. Did the BBC not realise the importance of Tamil, one of the five most widely spoken languages in the world, such a beautiful tongue that it was known, internationally, as the Latin of India? Did we not realise that to broadcast less than two hours a day in this pure and chaste language was derisory and insulting?

In vain we tried to ask him to get to the point. In vain we asked how on earth Tamil was one of the... It was useless. The professor would not stop. He used English words with delicious delight, and he used many of them.

At last, as he paused to cough, our chairman stood up and said that we were all delighted to meet and hear from such a distinguished figure, but now a full quarter of our time had been taken up and we would like to move on. Had Professor any views on, say, our handling of Kashmir, or the Middle East, or even the moving of Newshour?

The professor just about managed to master his cough and we caught the words "just a minute". We waited. "Anyone can cover these wretched unending current affairs and news nonsenses," said the professor, managing to jab with his stick. "But none – none has ever broadcast a programme so amusing, so enlightening, so efficacious in the teaching of the language of Shakespeare as this. And now we find we cannot hear it. It is a disgrace!"

A susurration of agreement went round the hall. We said we were sorry, but we did not understand. To exactly which BBC programme was Professor referring? Now he jabbed hard: "Just a Minute! Just a Minute, the panel show in which contestants are invited to talk about a subject without hesitation, deviation or repetition!" We sat there dumbfounded. Just a bloody Minute! Had it even been on the original schedule? There was no answer.

The professor turned to show himself to the audience, then addressed us again. "If the wonderful BBC, in all its wisdom, and with all its resources, does not care to bring Mr Mark Tully down to meet us, perhaps next time the BBC could bring here one of the greatest ever broadcasters in the English language. Mr Nicholas Parsons!"

He sat down to huge applause, and we pretended to take notes, and our media persons and our strategy persons nodded at each other, and seemed extremely hot.

Barry Langridge

"I Didn't Know Women Could Be so Crude"

A party from a Dutch journalism school was visiting Bush House, and some female students were sent up in a lift to meet me on the fourth floor. As the lift door opened, there was an explosion of screams and laughter, and the girls, red-faced and giggling, got out, leaving a tall young man (who worked in the French Service) to continue his journey upwards.

"What happened?" I asked the girls. When they calmed down, one of them said they had been pleased to be crammed into a lift with such a handsome man. Used to speaking freely in Dutch without fear of being understood, they spoke frankly about the attractions of this young man and what he might be like in more intimate circumstances. However, when the left arrived, he wished them a good day – in Dutch. "So embarrassing if he understood everything we said," commented one student.

I ran into the man soon afterwards. His mother was Dutch, he told me, and he had understood everything. He admitted he was flattered, but added: "I didn't know women could be so crude."

Hugh Closs

Our Radical New Format

A new programme organiser of the Persian Service wished to bring it up to date. Everybody knew that it had to be done, and weekday and Saturday programmes were soon rendered faster, livelier, and brighter – all in all, much more interesting for the listeners.

The Sunday evening programme was, however, another matter, for it was dominated, as it had been for aeons, by Professor Iqbal (not his real name), and everyone was either deeply respectful towards, or deeply frightened of, the professor.

On his first Sunday the new boss popped into Bush and went down to watch and listen to the programme. There was a bored studio manager in the cubicle, and in the little studio itself, across the glass, there were only two people.

The programme started with a little signature tune of Persian music, and then the younger of the two broadcasters said: "Welcome, dear listeners, to our Sunday offering. I will now read the news, and then we shall listen to, as usual, the thoughts of our own Professor Iqbal on a topical subject of the moment."

The youngster – he must have been about sixty – then read a nine-minute news, with no correspondents' voices or street sounds or music. He then said: "Professor Iqbal's topic for today is the strain between the North Atlantic Treaty Agency and the French government. Over to you now, dear Professor."

The programme being 29 minutes long, the professor then spoke for about 20 minutes. "Thank you, Professor Iqbal, for your insights. Farewell then, listeners. Till we meet across the airwaves once more." The signature tune was then played again by the listless studio manager.

"We cannot have this," the Persian programme organiser told his senior staff next day. "How can we compete with other radio services, let alone television, with stuff like that. We simply must have a more modern format. Next Sunday I want to hear more variety, more voices – including a woman's voice or two. I know you're afraid of Professor Iqbal, but if you don't do something I will close that programme completely, and politely end his tenure!" It was agreed that somebody would bell the cat.

On the next Sunday the boss went to the studio again. The same weary studio manager was at the controls, and in the cubicle were not two, but three people, and one of them was indeed a woman. A lively discussion perhaps?

The programme started. The woman welcomed listeners and said: "We have a slight change of format today, friends. I shall now read the world news, and then we shall have Mr Abbas and our own dear Professor Iqbal." The lady then read the news, and handed over to the professor, who said, "Today I shall be discussing the workings of the International Maritime Treaty, which is about to be reformed, and here to interview me about it is my young colleague Mr Abbas."

Mr Abbas: "Professor, could you kindly assess for our listeners the background, the ideals and the formation of the International Maritime Treaty." The professor then spoke for about 10 minutes, and then, to the boss' relief, stopped. Mr Abbas then spoke again: "Thank you, Professor Iqbal, could you now tell our listeners how, in your view, the International Maritime Treaty might at this week's conclave be reformed, and in what particular ways?" The professor then spoke again, for approximately another nine minutes. Then it was Mr Abbas's turn again. "Dear listeners, the clock has now caught up with us again: that is all we have time for this Sunday. Please do put pen to paper and tell us what you think about our radical new format. Until next week, farewell, and thank you again, Professor Iqbal."

The studio manager played the signature tune again, picked up his bag and left the studio, as did the new programme organiser, who had much to do.

Barry Langridge

Where Else but in Bush House?

When I came over from Chile as a young broadcaster to join the Latin American Service of the BBC in 1968, I never thought that in the summer of that year I would be in Lisbon with other 10 Bush House colleagues playing a football match against Portuguese broadcasters at the famous Benfica Stadium, in front of almost 60 thousand fans.

A few weeks earlier, Manchester United had played Benfica at Wembley in the final of the European Championship, which was widely covered by the media in Portugal and by the Portuguese Service. Prior to the game, visiting journalists came to Bush House for interviews and it was then decided that to celebrate the event it would

155

be a good idea to organise a football game between Bush House and the Portuguese broadcasters. It was to take place a few hours before the great final. Needless to say, the score was a massive win for the World Service team. But, since the visitors weren't very happy with the result, they invited the Bush House team to Lisbon for a return match, which was played at the Stadium of Light on a Saturday evening with the legendary Eusebio as a referee.

It was an incredible occasion. When we were taken to the football ground we could not believe the number of people going the same way, and never in our wildest dreams did we imagine there would be so many thousands at the game. We were only 11 players including, if I remember correctly, members of the World Service English, the Portuguese Service, the Latin American Service and one representative of the Israeli Section. Where else but in Bush House could this have ever happened? For those interested in the score, we lost 1 – 0.

Domingo Valenzuela

The Boss Learns About the Somalis

As times changed, along came the Internet and every language service wanted to slap their output up on their own page. Many services, especially those broadcasting to the toughest places (the Sri Lanka Tamils, the Burmese, the Central Asians), have large numbers of refugees or expats who can never go home and are unable to hear the direct transmissions. These smaller services seized on the net.

The management of the BBC, however, had their own ideas and tried to stop these entrepreneurs. Lists were drawn up of who should be the first – the Arabs, the Spaniards, the Persians, the Chinese, the Hindis and so on. But the Somalis, as is their wont, ignored all this nonsense and were the first at it. They were called to meetings: outraged strategists, technicians and people from finance waved their fingers. Our output should always be live; posting stuff on the net meant that people were seeing or hearing it late. Services must wait their turn.

However, the Somalis got lucky.

The new, energetic and gregarious director of the World Service travelled to Sydney for the Olympics. His tradition was never to travel in a BBC car, but to go with a local firm and learn from a local driver. When he got into a taxi he instantly asked the driver where he was from. He was a Somali.

The director mourned that his new friend could never have heard our famous Somali Service, because the signal could never get anywhere near here. "Of course I have – we listen to it every day. You are correct that we simply cannot hear the live broadcasts. But we always listen to the morning and evening programmes. My relative runs an Internet café. We all gather there for coffee and we all listen to the broadcasts together. There are many of us. It is our lifeline to home: also we learn about world affairs."

The director, on his return, decided to look at things again – and did. The Somalis were insufferable after that.

Barry Langridge

Childhood Visits

My early memories of visiting BVSH HOVSE date back to my childhood, as my father was a studio manager for the World Service in the 1980s, and I would often accompany him. I remember walking down long dark corridors for what seemed like miles, from one end of the building to a studio on another floor in another block. Some evenings we rarely came into contact with anybody else except for, maybe, someone at a drinks machine refilling a plastic cup of tea or coffee. My father would pick up his rota from a locker and plan his route from studio to studio like a London cabby to take the quickest path possible between jobs, which would sometimes include a dash across the courtyard if it wasn't raining.

Sometimes we visited the canteen, where I would be introduced to my father's colleagues who could speak up to 52 languages and had visited all corners of the globe. I was always impressed. It was great to be a kid sitting in studios with so many knobs and buttons, but I always had to resist the temptation to press anything – especially when they were live on air.

My father would often be managing a live news bulletin in Arabic. I remember the Arabs were always very friendly and would bring us drinks and sweets. Alternatively he would be pre-recording a show which would then need editing. We would go to another special suite, where I would watch him play with miles and miles of reel tape, editing out stammers, stutters, pauses, coughs and unnecessary noises. The big bins would be brimming with tape.

I feel privileged to have seen so many aspects of Bush House including the studio which housed all the sound effects objects for drama and music recordings. I saw the newly refurbished BBC Club and was there when they first started updating the studios by removing the old-fashioned reel-to-reels and replacing them with modern equipment.

It will be sad to see the World Service leave Bush House but the new building will, I'm sure, create a new wave of memories for other generations of children visiting their parents' workplace. I highly recommend it.

Gini Mitchell

Bush, the Love of My Life

I fell in love with Bush the day I set my eyes on him. So handsome, tall and warm that he is ready to embrace everyone who comes into his arms. Although his arms could protect me, sometimes I would get lost, especially on my way to a live transmission studio, when I joined the Burmese team in early 1994. I do not want to reveal my silly experiences — but I want to confess for the first and last time why I can never erase Bush out of my heart.

Ready to leave for a transmission, I would prepare myself not to get lost on my way to studio S35 from Centre Block, where the Burmese Section was, on the sixth floor. Once I followed my colleague so close behind him that I nearly ended up in a men's toilet room when he entered it, which made both of us very embarrassed, but I apologised and still waited for him in the corridor to keep following him. I simply couldn't afford to miss the transmission.

I have many nightmares, too, such as missing my transmission or finding that some of my scripts are left behind or having no idea where the studio is... But I am still like Alice in Wonderland, running around Bush, feeling secure as ever. There's a gym, for Bush always wants me to be in good shape, although I let him down by entering into the next-door bar, excusing myself with a wink: "I'm too exhausted, let me relax with a pint of beer, please, just for a couple of minutes." As a very forgiving and understanding big chap, Bush lets me enjoy a lovely evening with my mates from other language services and, of course, my close buddies from Studio Management.

Bush never wants me to leave him, and I believe in my heart of hearts that he arranges everything for me. A round-the-clock restaurant, a coffee counter on the first floor, an ATM machine, a gym, a bar with big sofas under dim lights with soft music, sometimes a happy hour accompanied by a live band; special Christmas meals and international festivities, such as Chinese and Vietnamese New Year in January and February, Thai and Burmese New Year in April, and Diwali. During the month of Ramadan, there are even special late meals. What more can you want from Bush, I wondered many times.

If I need a quiet break on my own or away from my boss, I can hide in the library, all peace and calm, reading my favourite books and newspapers or preparing my scripts. Will I still be as well looked after by Broadcasting House? I'm still reluctant to visit this new chap, for my love for Bush is too great.

I wish I could stay behind, clinging to his arms, but I know he doesn't want me to act like a teenager, madly and foolishly in love. He wants me to face the real world, to be a professional journalist with balanced editorial judgement, to go on adventurous foreign trips and to have confidence as a speaker at any functions, be it an Amnesty International event, a Burma-themed book launch or a discussion at a university. I would never have a chance to grow into someone like that on my own.

I can promise to the love of my life that I will never let you down, Bush, wherever I am, whomever I am with – I will never, ever forget the kind hospitality that you have showered upon me, I will always remember you standing high and mighty on Kingsway.

Nita Yin Yin May

An Imperial View From the Magic Corner

Bush House has become part of my identity and view of the world. We used to have a BBC shop at Bush where you could buy very cheap books. When I started working here I began filling my bookcase with travel books – and then there were my colleagues. I remember in the club there were maps of 60 different cities in the world. I found a lot of inspiration in those maps. Bush would give you a central view – from here you could look at the world and make comparisons. That was a magic corner for me: the BBC shop, the club, the travel agency, the Parker Pen shop, the café. I can exit the building through several doors but I always use the rear door. I want to cross that threshold before I go home to write.

Hai Lee

Dreams

I worked for the Arabic Service for 20 years. If Alice realised her dreams in the Wonderland, I realised my dreams in Bush House. I have not only written as a journalist but I have translated Shakespeare and Joyce. I am not wiser now but I can assure you, there is a difference.

Salah Niaz

Extraordinary Circadian Cycle

I think it was more than just a building – it was an organism in itself. Every day a night shift would melt away as the dawn came. We would often go and smoke cigarettes on the roof and watch everything along the Thames light up with the morning sun. Bush House would then steer into action as the first editors came in and early meetings started.

The news agenda really had a life of its own. There was this extraordinary circadian cycle. The building itself felt almost like an ancient monastery where religious rites were repetitively performed day after day.

That feeling of a huge cathedral is what I will take away from Bush House. There was something about the building that reminded me of my ancient college in Oxford, where we sang chorals every day. This ritualistic feel about the rhythm of Bush House may be religious for many of us.

Chris Gunness

Two Poems

God Rest You, Merry SDEs

God rest you, merry SDEs,
Let nothing you dismay.
The press review is eight lines short
and lead 2 is away.
The EDS has failed again
and Bowman's on his way.
Oh, why did you swap with Peter Shaw,
Peter Shaw?
Oh, why did you swap with Peter Shaw?

God rest you, merry SDEs,
The prospects are quite bleak.
They tell you that your brand new lead
Was used this time last week.
You hope things might improve
But then the tannoy starts to squeak.
And the club hasn't any sodding beer,
Sodding beer.
And the club hasn't any sodding beer.

God rest you, merry SDEs,
It isn't looking bright.
The dawn staff left a shambles
And the trolley's not in sight.
Your DE staggers in at last,
He's been up half the night.
But at least you earn forty grand a year,
Grand a year.
But at least you earn forty grand a year.

God rest you, merry SDEs,
There's worse to come we fear.
The copy taster's drunk again
And Princess Margaret's here.
The shift leader has just rung up,
She's got a poisoned ear.
Oh, thank God, you knock off at half past three,
Half past three.
Oh, thank God, you knock off at half past three.

God rest you, merry SDEs,
The confidence is nigh.
That highlight of the morning shift
When reputations die.
You're feeling very fragile
But they mustn't see you cry.
Oh, why can't they pick on someone new,
someone new?
Oh, why can't they pick on someone new?

God rest you, merry SDEs,
Some news has come along.
Our very own Bob Jobbins
Has been kidnapped in Hong Kong.
We use a quote from Austen Kark
But get his first name wrong.
Oh, next week you'll be back on NAB,
NAB.
Oh, next week you'll be back on NAB.

God rest you, merry SDEs,
This is a poor display.
Another eight corrections
Have just dropped in your tray.
Which, added to the seven kills,
Makes this a record day.
And you're still only up to C15,
C15.
And you're still only up to C15.
God rest you, merry SDEs,

*There's still two hours of strife
Before you leave the stinking ship
And trudge home to the wife.
Tomorrow you start dawns again,
Oh, what a fucking life.
And to think you could have worked for ITV,
ITV.
And to think you could have worked for ITV.*

Andy Moreton

Bosley's BBC Bequest

Some say you ranted, roared and raved,
Others that you burst into tears:
How did it feel when you were saved
The trouble of working four last years?
Let those who ask pin back their ears:
When my first wife gave up the fight
I poured a drink, said loudly Cheers
And played the Forty-eight all night.

And yet, dear Auntie as you were
But are no more, I cannot leave
Before I've given your spools a whirr
To hark back and a little grieve
For I have memories to weave
Of what was once a job for life
Of treasure no one can retrieve
As your own kin now wield the knife.

I call first one I never knew
Who like so many after him
Led two lives: one was getting through
To France when Europe's lights were dim,
The other was his mighty theme
Of Jonah in Bush House's whale.
Jean-Paul de Dadelsen his name:
His poem will outlive us all.

Keith Bosley

Epilogue

Farewell to Bush House

When the doors of Bush House finally close on the BBC World Service in July 2012, when those pillars that once welcomed the world as it approached along Kingsway fold their arms to it, when the marbled halls and lobbies fall silent, when the studio doors no longer shut with a sigh, when the friendly Babel chatter of a hundred voices in fifty tongues no longer fills the canteen, the final pages of the final chapter of a very special institution, World Service Bush House, will have been written. How special it was over its seven decades must be clear from the vivid testimonies of the preceding pages. They capture in micro detail the foibles, the accidents, the triumphs, the victories, the failures, the disappointments of more than two generations of broadcasting. They do so with wit, humour, honesty and self-deprecation as they reveal the skills, the courage, the resolution that were needed and that were so liberally offered in the service of the broadcasting that characterised World Service Bush House.

Why do I insist on that precise dual title inextricably linking the place, the building, the location with the broadcasts, the programmes, the broadcasters themselves? There is a danger in over-identifying a human organisation with the building in which it existed for so long and with such intimate intensity. The symbiotic relationship between place, purpose and behaviour can be overstated; but the paradoxical possibility that a building unsuited for broadcasting and journalistic activities actually released a synergistic rush of creativity cannot be ruled out. Nor can the strong feeling of many that the sheer eccentricity, the individuality of Bush House fortified the World Service's sense of itself. However you define it, World Service Bush House was real. In July 2012 it will cease to exist. That is a fact.

What happens next to the World Service as a department of the BBC is entire speculation. Everything depends on the extent to which the new all-embracing, fully funded relationship with the domestic BBC values, acknowledges and uses the World Service's historic qualities. In the past, the domestic BBC has frequently overlooked, under-appreciated, even patronised the World Service and its work. Can it do better now in a closer, more controlling relationship? The World Service's distinguished past deserves no less.

A farewell naturally requires, allows, a look back. An epilogue to a farewell asks for something more; an attempt at an explanation. That Bush House's journalists and broadcasters – see how easily the programming elides with and becomes described by the building! – spoke to their listeners as they did is history amply written and documented over 70 years. Why they did as they did, for so long, with such skill, with such determination under such hard circumstances, demands a different approach.

For the great historical periods of international politics seen by the World Service shaped it, influenced it, tested it and finally proved it. Born as an instrument for linking the British Empire, it soon found itself at the heart of the struggle with fascism during which it discovered that telling the truth was an essential commodity in the engagement with out-and-out propaganda. With fascism overcome, the world was torn by the Cold War, intense, ideological, with a terrifying overlay of military conflict and even the possibility of physical extermination. Some thought that communist ideology had to be directly fought with rebuttal and contradiction, the necessary weapons appropriate to a *journal de combat*. Others believed that making accurate news available to listeners and leaving it to them to draw their own conclusions was the only possible approach to be taken by a broadcaster from a liberal, plural, democratic nation. Wasn't "truth" itself – and the World Service dared to use the word – the strongest weapon?

While navigating the treacherous waters of decolonisation, the end of the Empire and non-alignment, all of which often tested the World Service's commitment to a world view as well as a British view, Bush House stayed anchored to the great BBC traditions of impartiality, accuracy and objectivity. The pay-off came when communism collapsed and the rather brief "new world order" followed. The Cold War propaganda stations, from Radio Moscow to Radio Beijing to Radio Free Europe/Radio Liberty, no longer had a reason for broadcasting. Their war was won – or lost – their purpose gone. The BBC World Service did not have to change ideological or theoretical gears – the commitment to offer listeners the information they needed to make sense of a noisy, confusing world was as it had always been.

If these were the great backdrops against which programmes were made and transmitted over a lifetime, what was the mindset of the people who made and delivered them? I risk a mighty set of generalisations in what follows, reassured at least by the fact that my own involvement in and understanding of World Service people covers the period from 1960, when I first worked at Bush House, to the present day, when I made two programmes of reminiscences with leading participants. My effort at understanding is offered as a mark of respect to those whom I knew and those of whom I only heard.

What questions mattered to World Service journalists and broadcasters? The terms of reference of their work were, without question, the whole world. This is not a mere phrase, a rhetorical claim. News could emerge from any place on the globe. Some parts of this vast canvas were more important than others. Few were so minor that the possibility of their never making the news occurred. There was a sense of duty – occasionally exaggerated – to report the obscure, to unearth the recherché, to value the recondite. These were the World Service's foibles, perhaps; its badges of difference, certainly; and infinitely preferable to dismissing the distant and the foreign because they were both distant and foreign.

Beyond that what mattered to World Service broadcasters was a sense of duty, which outsiders often found excessive; a commitment to be accurate, sometimes at the expense of being slower than others; an obligation to be truthful, avoiding what might be deemed "sensational", sometimes over-fastidiously; a determination to remain independent and a readiness to broadcast inconvenient truths, often to the governments of the target countries, sometimes to the British government itself.

What kind of people were they? The variety within Bush House was extraordinary, a joyful mixture of languages, cultures, outlooks and motivations. Some were exiles, some forced refugees, some former prisoners of their regime, some just British with a commitment to the wider world. Whoever they were, their broadly shared characteristics included a tendency to the serious, an inclination to the austere. In their more irritating modes they could be pious, self-righteous and downright superior to those who were judged to work to less exacting standards. Yet much of this was forgiveable. "Bushmen" – the then acceptable collective noun – worked with few resources but lots of compensating principles. They knew they were poor – and indeed they were – but they tried to be honest. And everyone knew they were part of the BBC, which kept them journalistically and editorially independent of the Foreign and Commonwealth Office, the World Service's historic paymasters. For they were, first and last, journalists and not surrogate diplomats.

What kept them going under the difficult circumstances they faced: financial cuts at home, jamming abroad, political pressure everywhere? The belief, underpinned by strongly shared values, that they were broadcasting on the grounds of principle rather than seeking popularity or large audiences, welcome as they were. The knowledge, constantly acquired, that their broadcasts and programmes really mattered to their listeners. The evidence that listeners in many parts of the world needed the programmes so much that they risked freedom or even life to tune in and listen. The experience that their programmes could influence politics thousands of miles away and that they were often proved to be accurate and right.

Such were the compensations of broadcasting into the vast short-wave ether. The broadcasts continued, whether or not such compensations were immediately available or not.

Why did this matter to the rest of the BBC? Despite the prevailing, usually affectionate view of Bush House as peopled by amiable but well-intentioned and well-informed eccentrics, deeper down the domestic BBC recognised that the World Service offered a genuinely broader view of the world. If, viewed from Broadcasting House, foreign news was an occasional eruption stuck on to the primary, often hermetic carapace of the domestic and local scene, the world view from Bush House was one where no news was foreign; it was all news of the world, always of the world. This was and remains a crucial distinction in perspective, which mattered and should matter to the entire BBC.

Bush House contained and offered an incredible body of knowledge, expertise and insights instantly, freely and generously available anywhere and to anyone in the BBC. "Crisis in Ouagadougou? Call Bush!" was the cry, and a hundred such like. What was offered, what was available was a far closer, richer, deeply informed connection with the global audience for the entire BBC broadcast output.

Why did the BBC World Service matter to the government which paid for it for almost 80 years, mainly through the Foreign and Commonwealth Office grant-in-aid? The World Service was the most successful and most reliable international broadcaster; research said so, anecdotage said so, our competitors said so. It was trusted by listeners because it not only aimed to be independent of its paymaster, Her Majesty's Government – it was heard to be independent, sometimes embarrassingly so. No other broadcaster enjoyed such an arm's-length – sometimes complex – relationship with its governmental funder. In return, Britain gained the reputational benefit of a working example of the "British way"; an official broadcaster who did not broadcast propaganda. For its critics, it was always "British hypocrisy" at work; but they still listened. It was the only credible "hypocrisy" on the radio dial. "In a world of lies," was an occasional critical comment, "you tell fewer. Of course we know where the BBC stands; it is a British perspective. But you are more reliable."

Did the World Service matter to the nation? Most of it never heard it, could not receive it – sometimes being told they shouldn't even try to listen to it! – and were only dimly aware that they paid for it. Many resident expats, indeed, just wished they could get Radio 4. To the extent that British listeners were aware of the BBC World Service – and many listened in the wee small hours, or came across it while abroad – they strongly valued what it did and what they saw it stood for. Those values included being a very public example of the British sense of fair play: "We will tell others uncomfortable things about ourselves even if it hurts." It demonstrated the British ability to master a paradox: "We pay you but we don't tell you what to say." It was based on the belief that the what and why you broadcast is more important than the how. It was seen as a "great British cultural export", part of the "British way of life", and for some a reminder of how you could maintain the old standards. In fact, once you probed, the wellspring of admiration and affection for the BBC World Service ran very deep in national public opinion. They sensed as well as knew that it was a "good thing" and said so when asked.

One further characteristic must not be forgotten; Bush House's capacity to fight for its continuance, possibly for its survival. When faced with government cuts or service closures, Bush House traditionally used every stratagem and tactic it could summon, called every friend it could enlist. Often it succeeded even when such public fights were not convenient to the domestic BBC. But they were needed because Bush House felt it was standing up for values that belonged to its journalists, its broadcasters, its engineers and, above all, to its listeners. It was never ashamed of the fight or frightened of taking it up.

If the qualities of a World Service person are to be summed up, I suggest they include the following: endurance; stubbornness; belief in principle; flexibility without fundamental compromise. All combined to deliver an extraordinary degree of job and life satisfaction. As one former colleague put it very precisely, "What was really important was how needed we were by our listeners; we were a source that no one else produced. It is not often in life that you do a job that contributes to knowledge, well-being and contact with the outside world for others." Another former colleague said: "During the Cold War it was always said that we 'kept hope alive'. How lucky I was to have a job that was so worth doing."

So World Service Bush House falls silent, the studios stripped, the doors closed, the living presence ended. The dogs bark and the lovely, motley, raucous, passionate, straggly caravan moves on. May its next resting place give it a warm welcome.

John Tusa

Acknowledgements

We are indebted to all those who contributed their stories, photographs and drawings to make this publication possible. John Tusa, Gwyneth Williams and Hugh Saxby kindly agreed to be our critical readers, checking the draft and making useful suggestions along the way. Their wholehearted endorsements are invaluable, and we are very grateful to them for their support. We also thank Anna Horsbrugh-Porter, William Crawley, Hugh Lunghi, Rizwana Rahmani, Lisa Petit and Anna McGovern for their help with this book. Many thanks are due also to The Open University and the Centre for Research on Socio-Cultural Change for funding the research on which this book is partly based.

Hamid Ismailov, Marie Gillespie, Anna Aslanyan